Injury
Time

Alan Gibbons is a full-time writer and a visiting speaker and lecturer at schools, colleges and literary events nationwide, including the major book festivals: Edinburgh, Northern Children's Book Festival, Swansea, Cheltenham, Sheffield and Salford. Alan has recently embarked on a high profile, nationwide campaign to champion libraries and librarianship and to reevaluate government commitment to educational spending.

Also by Alan Gibbons:

FOOTBALL TITLES
Julie and Me and Michael Owen Makes Three
Total Football series:
Some You Win . . .
Under Pressure
Divided We Fall
Last Man Standing
Power Play
Twin Strikers
Final Countdown

HORROR TITLES
Hell's Underground:
Scared to Death
The Demon Assassin
Renegade
Witch Breed

FANTASY TITLES
The Legendeer Trilogy:
Shadow of the Minotaur
Vampyr Legion
Warriors of the Raven

The Legendeer Trilogy (3-in-1)

The Darkwing:
Rise of the Blood Moon
Setting of a Cruel Sun

The Darkwing Omnibus (2-in-1)

REAL LIFE THRILLERS
The Lost Boys' Appreciation Society
Blood Pressure
The Edge
Caught in the Crossfire
The Defender

Injury
Time

Alan Gibbons

Orion
Children's Books

First published in Great Britain in 1998
by Orion Children's Books
Reissued in Great Britain in 2010
by Orion Children's Books
a division of the Orion Publishing Group Ltd
Orion House
5 Upper St Martin's Lane
London WC2H 9EA
An Hachette UK company

JF

The Orion Publishing Group's policy is to use papers that are natural,
renewable and recyclable products and made from wood grown in
sustainable forests. The logging and manufacturing processes are expected
to conform to the environmental regulations of the country of origin.

978-1-4440-0179-2

A catalogue record for this book is available from the British Library.

www.orionbooks.co.uk

Rough Diamonds

THE SQUAD

Darren 'Daz' Kemble (goalkeeper)
Joey Bannen (defence and substitute goalkeeper)
Mattie Hughes (defence)
Anthony 'Ant' Glover (defence)
Jimmy Mintoe (defence)
Carl Bain (defence)
John O'Hara (midfield)
Jamie Moore (striker)
Kevin 'Guv' McGovern (midfield and captain)
Bashir Gulaid (midfield)
Pete 'Ratso' Ratcliffe (midfield)
Dave Lafferty (striker)
Gordon Jones (defence)

Manager: Ronnie Mintoe

PART ONE

An Injury To One ...

One

Some people have all luck. Dave Lafferty, for one.

Between the two of us, it's me and Dave who make the Diamonds tick. Sure, we've got plenty of cracking players, but without the pair of us something would definitely be missing. The way I see it, the Rough Diamonds are a team with two hearts, which is just as well because the estate where we live – the Diamond in the north end of Liverpool – is a boring dump with no heart at all. Anyway, about the two hearts. There's me, Kev McGovern, the Guv'nor. I captain the side. Midfield general, grafter, spoiler, creator. You name it, I'll do it. The point about me is that I'm a one-hundred-percenter. My team is my crusade. My team strip is my religion. Which makes each match part of a holy war. I tell you, I give my all ... then some. My opponent may be a better player, a Pele, a Keegan, a Cantona, a Ronaldo, a football genius. I don't care. Most times, I'll still come out on top. It's the hunger, you see. It's always there, this gnawing pain inside me. All my life I've had people telling me I'm nobody, a loser. Well, they can say what they like. There's one thing I do know, I'll never go down without a fight.

Dave's different. Everything I have to work for, everything I have to practice and try over and over again, is effortless for him, it just comes naturally. We read about this Greek feller in school once, Achilles or something. The gods dipped him in a magic river when he was a baby, and it turned him into a sort of superhero. Colossal strength, fantastic bravery, you know the scene. A kind of atomic Gladiator. Not the sort of geezer to tangle with. The way I see it, there's a sporting heaven somewhere with a big, shining river running right through it and these gods must have come along and dipped our Davey in the waters. How else do you explain a kid who's brilliant at everything? I mean, I love footy. Eat it, breathe it, sleep it – I live for it – but only footy. It's my passion. My only one. I couldn't care less about any of these other sports. They're just distractions. I'm bored stiff all summer, waiting for August and the first kick-off. The close season's a complete nightmare. If you ask me, June, July and August are a one-hundred-day prison sentence with a football-shaped hole through the middle. Not for Dave. He's great at athletics, brilliant at rounders, swims like a fish, excels at cricket. And he's good at his school work. Makes you sick, doesn't he?

Come to think of it, I always thought Dave was even better than this Achilles character. Achilles had a problem, you see. When the gods dipped him in that river, they had to hang on to him somewhere, so his heel never got dipped. And that's how his enemies did him in. They found his weakness and shot him through the heel. That's why Dave had one over on old Achilles. He didn't have a weakness. The jammy beggar is good at everything. I was jealous, I suppose. It didn't matter how hard I work, how many hours I banged a ball against the community centre wall, I was always outshone by Lucky Dave Lafferty.

If I scored a couple of goals, he'd get a hat-trick. If I beat my man, he'd go round two of them. It wasn't just that he was a football hero, either. He's always been happy in a way I'll never be. You should see him out with his mum and dad. His parents actually hold hands. And that's after being married for fifteen years! Mine split up ages ago. Put them together in one room and it's like a rotten civil war. Honestly, as we came to the end of our first season in the South Sefton Junior League, I would have given my right arm to swap places with Dave. Come to think of it, I'd have given both arms! It sounds awful, I know, but I suppose I was half hoping he did have an Achilles heel, after all. I don't wish him any harm, of course. He's a mate. But just for once it would have been nice to see that he was human like the rest of us.

That's where the enemy came in. Luke Costello and Andy 'Brain Damage' Ramage. Unlike me, they did wish Dave harm. And how! They're a pair of real low-lifes. Costello's the brains. Brain Damage – you can spot him by the way he drags his knuckles on the ground – provides the muscle. They hate the Diamonds, you see, every one of us, but most of their hatred is directed at yours truly. Costello and Brain Damage are the sort who have to tread all over somebody else so they can walk tall, putting the frighteners on anybody who seems weaker than them. They want to be cocks of the estate but I keep getting in their way. They've tried taking me head on and failed.

A couple of months back, Costello came up with this master plan to get the Diamonds knocked out in the Challenge Cup semi-final, only we rumbled them. So he had to watch while we beat Ajax Aintree, one of the best sides in the league. He must have been really choked. Then after the match I went and rubbed his nose in it even further. I shouted his name and when he turned round I drove the ball smack in his face, and there's a bit of power in this right peg of mine. I didn't half enjoy it, watching his stupid head snap back. As I watched him crawling away with his lousy mates, I knew he'd be really sore, but I didn't care. We were through to the Cup final, and that's what mattered. In the back of my mind, though, this voice was telling me not to relax, not to take my eye off the poison pair even for a second. They would be determined to get at me another way. But little did I know how successful they would be. Little did I know that they'd be the ones to find Dave's weak spot and use it against the Diamonds.

Two

Dave squatted on his haunches and watched the celebrations. They'd done well, but he wasn't completely swept along with the euphoria. By his own standards, the Challenge Cup semi-final had been a pretty ordinary performance. He'd held the line up front for most of the game and set up two of the goals in Jamie Moore's winning hat-trick. Yes, definitely ordinary.

'Did you see what Daz did?' Jimmy Mintoe was saying. 'I mean, whoever heard of an attacking goalie?'

'And what about Jamie?' laughed Kev. 'A hat-trick. That's some way to mark your return to the side.'

'So who do we play in the final?' asked Gordon Jones.

It wasn't difficult to work out what he was thinking. In Ajax Aintree they'd beaten a side four points clear in the race for the league title. Surely the Diamonds had nothing to fear from anyone else?

'The final!' said Joey Bannen, as if he'd never dared mention the possibility before. He rolled the words on his tongue like the sweetest of toffees. 'We'd better take a look at our opponents.'

'That's a point,' said Kev. 'I'm not even sure who we'll be playing.' He glanced at Ronnie Mintoe, their manager.

'Sorry, lads,' said Ronnie, 'I've got to get our Michael to *his* match now.'

Michael was Ronnie's eighteen-year-old son. He watched most of the Diamonds' matches from his wheelchair.

'Come on, Mike,' said Ronnie, giving the wheelchair a push over a troublesome divot.

'But who do we play in the final?'

Michael laughed. 'Why not ask the oracle?'

The oracle was a scrawny bag of bones by the name of Peter Ratcliffe, Ratso to his mates. What he didn't know about football could be written on the back of a silicon chip.

'Only one way to find out,' said Ratso. 'It looks like they're still playing over the far side. Follow me.'

'Oh, come on, Ratso,' moaned Ant Glover. 'You must know. Don't keep us in suspenders. Who is it?'

Ratso gave a superior smile and led the way across the playing-field.

'Anyway,' said Joey Bannen as he tagged along. 'What's this match Mike's off to?'

'He does that wheelchair basketball,' said Kev. 'Haven't you noticed his arms? Muscles like bags of grapefruit.'

'Want to know who we're playing, do you?' asked Ratso, interrupting their conversation. 'Well, here they are.'

By the look on his face, Ratso had a surprise in store. He didn't disappoint. Stopping suddenly, he stabbed a bony finger towards Pitch Five.

'Oh, not that lot again,' groaned Gord, seeing the green-and-white hooped shirts in front of him.

'Longmoor Celtic,' groaned John O'Hara. 'I hope they don't get through.'

Kev ignored the fainthearts alongside him. 'What's the score, mate?' he asked one of the dads on the touch-line.

'Six-three.'

'Who to?'

'Who do you think? My lad's side, Celtic.'

John lowered his eyes and shook his head. 'Typical.'

He was a hundred proof grump. He'd find something to complain about in heaven.

'Oh, shut up, misery,' said Kev.

'How long to go?' asked Jimmy.

The dad consulted his watch. 'The ref should blow any time now. We were late getting started. Some of the St Bede's boys were caught in traffic on the East Lancs. Lights were out, or something.'

'Longmoor flipping Celtic,' sighed John. 'It might as well be Juventus for all the chance they'll give us.'

'Behave,' said Ant. 'They're nothing special.'

'Oh no?' said Ratso. 'If that's what you think then you've got a short memory.' He was referring to their league encounter, a bruising affair that went the Diamonds' way three-two.

'We won, didn't we?' demanded Ant.

'Yeah,' said John, his usual gloomy self, 'by the skin of our teeth.'

'They battered us for most of the game,' said Ratso. 'You can't say they didn't.'

'Whose side are you on, anyway?' asked Ant, rounding on him. 'Since when did you stick up for Grumbling John?'

'I'll tell you who I stick up for,' Ratso said. 'The Diamonds. No axes to grind. I'm a team player. I don't agree with John making out Longmoor are invincible, but we'd be stupid to under-estimate them. If there's a side in this league who could pip Ajax for the championship, you're looking at it.'

'Ratso's right,' said Dave. 'Just look how they defend.'

St Bede's were making a forward run, but their progress came to a halt as a tall mid-fielder put in a strong physical challenge.

'That lad rings a bell,' said Jimmy.

'Nosmo,' said Gord ruefully. 'I remember him, all right.'

John 'Nosmo' King was the Longmoor skipper. He was a first year at Scarisbrick High and twelve months older than the Diamonds who were still in Year Six. The extra year's growth showed. Nosmo had the strength to shrug off the St Bede's player and come away with the ball in one controlled movement.

'We'll have our work cut out,' Dave observed. 'We caught them by surprise last time. They won't fall for the same tricks twice.'

'So what *do* we do?' grunted Ant. 'Lie down and die?'

'Don't be soft,' scolded Kev. 'The Diamonds are fighters. We do our homework, we put in the time on the training-field and we push them every inch of the way.'

'*Then* we get beaten,' said John.

'Oh, shut him up, somebody,' said Ant, 'or I'll do it the hard way.'

Just then the whistle went and the lads in green-and-white raised their arms in a victory salute.

'They'll walk the final,' said the dad. 'I was talking to the manager. He nipped across for a few minutes to watch the opposition. Bunch of two-bit scallies. Beats me how they won against a class outfit like Ajax.'

'We,' Kev announced pointedly, 'are the opposition.'

The dad didn't show any embarrassment. He didn't even flinch. 'Still down the bottom end of the league, aren't you, lads?'

'Yes, so?'

'So our John's lot are challenging for the championship. They've been up there all season snapping at Ajax's heels, and now they're only four points adrift.

And they've still got to play them. Could be a Championship decider.'

'So what?' said Ratso, determined to bring the boastful dad back down to earth. 'We beat them a few weeks ago.'

'It won't happen again,' said the dad. 'You took our lads by surprise. They'll hammer you in the final. Be warned, our John says they're really up for it.'

'Get lost,' snarled Ant, but Gord butted in immediately.

'John,' he asked. 'John who?'

'John King. Why?'

The Diamonds went quiet. They realized that they were talking to Nosmo's dad, of all people.

'Hello,' came a voice. 'Meeting the opposition, are you, Dad?'

Talk of the devil. It was Nosmo himself.

'We'll have you, Diamonds.'

'In your dreams,' retorted Guv. 'We've thumped you once, remember.'

'Thumped is the word for it,' said Nosmo, glaring at Gord. 'You're the dirtiest side we've played this season. You only won by kicking us off the pitch.'

'What are you on about?'

'He knows.' Nosmo was staring fixedly at Gord.

Gord re-lived his marrow-jarring collision with the Celtic attacker. 'That was an accident.'

'Yes, sure,' snorted Nosmo, eyeing the Diamonds' central defender with undisguised hostility. 'And I'm Pamela Anderson.'

Some of his team-mates chortled appreciatively.

'Like to have a bet on the outcome this time?' asked Nosmo.

Ratso went bright red. They'd had a bet last time round, only Ratso had had to borrow fifteen pounds out of his mum's purse to do it. Without permission. He had got into real hot water for that little escapade. 'No bets,' he said. 'We'll sort this out on the football field.' He paused, staring into Nosmo's eyes. 'Come to think of it, we've got two bites of the cherry.'

One of Nosmo's team-mates nudged him and handed him a fixture list. Nosmo glanced down and gave a low whistle. 'Well, well. You're right, we've still got another meeting in the league before the final. Better get yourselves a spade, lads, because we're going to bury you. Both times.'

'No chance,' said Guv. 'We turned you over once, and we'll do it again.'

'Never in a million years.'

'Oh no?' said Guv. 'So who's going to stop us?'

Little did the Diamonds know, but at that very moment the answer just might have been standing on the other side of Jacob's Lane.

'All right, Luke, so what happened to your clever plan?' asked Brain Damage. 'I told you we should have just done them while we had the chance.'

'Oh, grow up,' snapped Costello. 'McGovern would love that. He can handle you any time, Andy. He's done it often enough.'

'He got lucky,' said Brain Damage.

'You make your own luck,' said Costello. There was a touch of contempt in his voice that got under Brain Damage's skin.

'Meaning?'

'The point is,' said Costello, ignoring Brain Damage, 'we're not going to get one over on McGovern and his crew without showing a bit of nous.'

'You said that last time.'

'And,' Costello told him, 'I'll keep saying it until you

get it through your thick skull. We'll need more than the old knuckle to sort out McGovern. If you go face-to-face with him, you're fighting on his terms. No, we need to come up with something better.'

'Like what?' asked Tez Cronin. He'd always been Brain Damage's right-hand man. Then along came Costello to take over leadership of the gang. Which made Tez the right-hand man's right-hand man. He felt the demotion keenly, but not as keenly as Brain Damage. It's no fun being an ex-leader.

'I'm thinking,' said Costello. He looked around his gang. His old mate Jelly Wobble was there, and as well as Brain Damage and Tez, there were three other boys. Enough to be a thorn in McGovern's flesh, but enough to make him crack? Costello didn't think so, somehow. It was the shouts from the match still being played on the pitch that gave him an idea.

'What does McGovern care about most in the world?' he wondered out loud.

'Dunno,' said Brain Damage.

Costello rolled his eyes. Damage by name, damage by nature.

The gesture irritated Brain Damage. Costello didn't miss a chance to stamp his authority – usually on Brain Damage's face. 'Oh, how should I know? The Diamonds, I suppose.'

Costello nodded. 'Exactly, and that's how we get back at him. We find the weak link.'

'Meaning?'

'Meaning we wreck the team.'

Costello took in the puzzled faces of the gang. 'Oh, what are you like? McGovern's got his heart set on the Challenge Cup, hasn't he?'

'Ye-es,' said Brain Damage, still wondering where all this was leading.

'Don't you see? If we can just stop them winning the Cup, they'll collapse like a pack of cards. Then we can get them at each other's throats. After that it's bye bye McGovern.'

Suddenly Brain Damage was smiling. 'And hello us.' Life would be the way it had been before McGovern arrived on the scene. Brain Damage could see it already. Throwing his weight around, nicking stuff off the wimps, basking in the sheer fright on his victims' faces. He'd be cock of the estate again. A greedy smirk spread across his face.

Costello grinned too. 'You up for it, then?'

'Try holding me back.'

'That's more like the Andy Ramage we all know and love.'

'But what do we actually *do*?' asked Tez.

Costello rubbed his chin. 'For starters, we need a full list of their team.'

'Me and Tez can work that out,' said Brain Damage. 'McGovern and Jamie Moore go to Cropper Lane. The rest are at Our Lady's. My cousin goes there. He'll know them all.'

'Good,' said Costello. 'You get on to him. Then we need a fixture list. I should have one at home. After all, I'm still registered as a player for Blessed Hearts.'

'Then?' asked Brain Damage.

'Then,' said Costello, stroking the side of his face where Guv's purposefully-aimed ball had struck him. 'We smash them.'

Three

That Dave Lafferty, he's one jammy beggar. I tell you, you could drop him off the top of Blackpool Tower and he'd land on his feet and walk away. We were just giving Longmoor Celtic a bit of verbal last Sunday morning when along came George Rogan. He runs the South Sefton Junior League, but that's not why we try to catch his eye whenever he's around. No, George isn't just the League secretary, he's a scout for Everton. If he spots any promising players, he gives the club the nod. Impress George Rogan and you could be taking the first step to a YTS with the Blues.

And that's just what Dave's been doing, impressing him. Anyway, George came over and collared Ronnie, our manager. You know what he said? Dave reminded him of a younger version of Mark Hughes. Now that's some comparison. Mark Hughes has played for Man United, Barcelona and Chelsea. I could see the similarities right away. Dave leads from the front and intimidates defenders with his strength. He's the ace target man, shielding the ball with his back to the goal then spraying out telling passes. What's more, he's got two good feet and heads the ball like an educated sea lion. He's not that tall but he can put up with a bit of rough handling and give as good as he gets. I've seen defenders climbing all over him and he just leans into them and shrugs them out of the way.

Me, Ant and Bashir were green with envy. And when George asked if he could talk to Dave's mum and dad, we went even greener. Dave was going to get a trial. It was obvious. We watched him. He'd gone bright red with embarrassment, but he was proud and excited, too. It was something we all dreamed about, taking the field with a Premiership club. It was a passport to heaven. Your own flash car with your name on the side, loads of money, and the worship of tens of thousands of adoring fans.

It's not fair. I mean, that's my future he's got. Just look at the pair of us, for goodness sake. Dave's already got it all. His parents are still an item and they're both working so they can take him everywhere. Alton Towers last weekend and it's Oasis in August. There isn't a sport he isn't good at and he's dead brainy at school. Then there's me. Parents split up. Dad missing most of the time and Mum struggling to drag me and our Gareth up on Bosnia street. No money, no holidays, no rotten anything. And on top of that, most of the teachers and a couple of the local coppers think I should be buried in a sand bucket. An unexploded bomb, that's me. So who gets the break? Lucky Lafferty, as per pigging usual. I tell you, I'd have crawled over razor wire for a chance like Dave's. Like I said, he's one jammy beggar.

Four

Dave was ringing the front doorbell the way a hamster runs round its exercise wheel. He was demented with excitement.

Ding ding ding …

Dixie, the family's cocker spaniel, started yapping happily. Dave smiled in expectation of the dog's welcome. His mother's voice filtered through the barking. 'Dixie, Dixie, hush. Hang on, Davey.'

Hang on? No way.

Ding ding ding …

Woof woof woof.

'I said: hang on. Oh, can it, Dixie.'

But Dave had seen the future and it was Lafferty-shaped.

Ding ding ding …

Woof woof woof.

'Oh, for crying out loud.'

Her feet were stamping down the stairs.

Mu-um. Come on.

Ding ding ding.

Woof woof woof.

This is important. It's life or death.

At last the door swung open. Dixie exploded up at Dave, his entire body shaking and wriggling with joy at his master's return.

'You'll wear that bell out one of these days,' Mum grumbled. 'What is it with you, anyway?'

'I've got something to tell you!' Dave blurted out as he wrestled with the blur of affection that was Dixie.

'Not before I've had a word with you,' Mum interrupted.

Dave saw the roll of bin-bags in her hand. She was spring cleaning.

'But this is important.'

'So's this.' Mum waved an apple core under his nose. It had fur on it. Dixie sniffed at it hopefully then backed off.

That room of yours,' she said. 'It isn't a room, it's a ...'

'Bomb site?' Dave had decided to help her out. It would be quicker in the long run. 'Pigsty?'

'Pigsty isn't the word for it,' stormed Mum. 'If you poured all the muck from every pigsty in the known universe, then mixed it with a month's rubbish from Sefton dump you might be close. Dixie's kennel is tidier than your pit.'

'I think you're exaggerating a bit there, Mum.'

Dixie's eyes were darting from Mum to Dave, as though he understood what they were saying.

'Not that much,' said Mum, determined to sound

stern. 'Do you have any idea how many pairs of undies you had stuffed under your mattress?'

'Six?' Dave suggested helpfully.

'Five,' said Mum with a warning glare. He wasn't meant to take this so lightly. 'Five pairs of undies and three odd socks. It's a wonder they didn't walk by themselves. That'll be the reason you never have any clothes.'

'I have got clothes,' said Dave. 'I left my school uniform on the bookcase.'

'And that's another thing,' fumed Mum. 'That was supposed to be in the wash on Friday evening, not stuffed in there with your footy mags. How am I supposed to have it washed and dried for the morning?'

Dave scratched behind Dixie's ears and smiled. 'You'll find a way, Mum. You're a marvel.' He winced inside. He couldn't believe he'd said anything so naff, but he had to shut her up for a moment. It worked. Suddenly she was lost for words.

'I've got a bit of news,' he said quickly before she had a chance to recover. 'George Rogan thinks he could get me a trial with Everton. He wants to talk to you and Dad.'

In the following seconds there were only two sounds. The energetic thump of Dixie's tail and Mum's tongue being well and truly tied.

'He's here,' said Dave excitedly.

Mum was at his side, simultaneously peering through the net curtains and pushing Dixie away from the window. 'Right,' she said. 'Don't tell him straight away. We'll drop a few hints and see how long it takes before he cottons on.'

'The hunter returns,' Dad announced grandly as he held up a large carrier bag.

'Hunter,' snorted Mum. 'You couldn't hunt a sausage. You mean you dropped in at the supermarket on the way home.'

'A complete ready-cooked roast chicken, a box of wickedly fattening chocolates and a bottle of your better-than-average French plonk,' Dad said, dismissing her sarcasm. 'And I didn't have to go near the supermarket to get it.'

He deposited the food and the wine on the telephone table and hung up his coat.

'How do you know it's French?' asked Dave.

'Because it's wearing a striped T-shirt and a beret,' said Dad.

'Come again?'

'I'm kidding. It says so on the label, mastermind.'

'So where *did* this lot come from?' asked Mum.

'I won it,' said Dad. 'Raffle at the club.' He meant the North Liverpool Harriers, his cycling club.

'Oh well,' said Mum, carrying the chicken into the kitchen. 'That's dinner sorted out.'

'Any news?' asked Dad, fighting his way past Dixie.

Mum and Dave exchanged glances.

'News, news,' mused Mum. 'Now, did we have any news, Davey?'

'Can't think of anything,' said Dave. By way of preparation for the big announcement, he'd changed into his Everton away strip.

'What are you two up to?' asked Dad.

'Up to,' said Mum. 'Us?'

Dave assumed the same air of mock-innocence. Even Dixie gave it a try, but it wasn't very convincing. It never is from a dog.

'Yes, you two. What gives?'

Dave wandered over to the radio cassette and casually switched it on. Like he hadn't had it on pause for half an hour. The 'Match of the Day' theme blasted out.

'So that's it,' said Dad. 'You won today.'

'Three-two,' said Dave. 'We'll be playing Longmoor Celtic in the final.'

'Score any?'

'No, but I made a couple.'

'Right,' said Dad. 'Now I know your news, let's get that dinner on. I'm partial to a bit of chicken and that plonk will go down a treat.'

Mum rested a hand on his shoulder. 'The match wasn't the news, Phil. Shall we tell him, Dave?'

'Tell me what?'

Dave tugged at the Everton shirt with both hands. 'Only that I could end up wearing this for real.'

Dad stared. He still didn't understand.

'I've got a trial, Dad. Mr Rogan came up to me and Ronnie after the game—'

'Who's this Mr Rogan?' asked Dad, interrupting.

'Only a scout for Everton,' said Dave. 'He wants to come and have a chat with you. He thinks I show promise.'

'What?' said Dad. 'As a footballer?'

'No,' said Dave with gentle sarcasm, 'as a lion tamer.'

'But what about university?' asked Dad.

'What *about* university?' said Mum. 'The lad is still only eleven, you know. I think you're jumping the gun a bit.'

Dave winced. His dad had started work at sixteen and he didn't want Dave to be the same.

'But a professional footballer? I'm not sure.'

Dave couldn't believe his ears. He'd thought Dad would be over the moon. Over the sun, even.

'Phil,' Mum said, giving her husband a look. 'We're

not talking serious career options yet. This is a first trial. Davey is really excited. Don't spoil it.'

Dave looked hopefully at Dad.

'OK, OK, we'll see what this feller has to say for himself. I'm not signing anything, though.'

'I don't think we have to,' said Mum. 'It's just a first contact with the club.'

'But wouldn't it be brill, Dad?' asked Dave. 'Me playing for Everton!'

'There's a long way to go before we can talk seriously about that happening,' said Dad. He still didn't seem too keen on the idea. 'Hundreds of lads must get disappointed along the way.'

'But it could happen,' said Dave. 'Couldn't it, Mum?'

'Of course it could, son,' she replied, trying to make up for her husband's lukewarm response. 'It's one of the things that makes life worthwhile. Every now and then dreams do come true.'

Five

'We'd better start without them,' said Ronnie. He'd given Carl and Mattie long enough. 'Honestly, you lads. If you're not getting the hump and walking out on me, then you're giving training a miss. I bet kids don't act like this in Blundellsands.'

'I bet they don't care about footy in Blundellsands,' observed Ratso. 'Too busy polishing their jewellery.' He had a point. Estates like the Diamond have always been a nursery of talent for the beautiful game.

'It'd still be nice if you were a bit less ... sparky.'

'Sparky,' chuckled Ratso as he looked round his

team-mates. 'That's a polite word for it.' Their engines ran on pure aggression.

Kev peered through the mist and drizzle of the cold April evening. Across the dismal wasteland of the Diamond nothing was moving. Even the stray dogs had somewhere better to go. Kev clenched and unclenched his fists. He'd kill Carl and Mattie for this.

'I never thought anybody would be missing tonight,' said Gord. 'Not after what we did yesterday.'

'Too right,' Ratso agreed. 'If you've just done the hard bit getting through the semi-final, you'd expect the whole team to be fired up. Can't say I'm that surprised at Carl and Mattie, though. They're as much use as rubber toilet paper.'

'They were big mates of yours once,' Daz observed.

'That's before they started sniding off on Gord,' Ratso replied. He didn't like being reminded that he'd once been in league with the team's most shifty and unreliable members.

Kev snorted and spat on the turf. He'd never had much time for Carl and Mattie but they were part of the squad so he'd gone easy on them. Not any more. They'd just broken the unwritten law – you don't let your mates down.

For that he was considering breaking their necks. Slowly, deliberately, painfully. 'Yes, let's get on with it,' he agreed, his voice little more than a menacing growl. 'I'll sort that pair of lamebrains later.'

Ronnie gave him a long, hard look. Captain or not, he didn't want Kev sorting anybody. The Diamonds' manager was usually an easy-going sort. 'Gather round, lads,' he said. 'I've just found out that Anthony here has been hiding his light under a bushel. I caught him practising round the back of the changing-rooms.'

'Come again?' asked Joey.

'He's got a secret talent,' said Ratso helpfully.

'Oh.'

'So what is it?' asked Jamie. Ant was his cousin and he thought he knew everything about him.

'Show him, Ant,' said Ronnie. 'Defenders, take up your positions. You're defending a forward run into the last third.'

The Diamonds defence spread across the penalty area. Daz skipped up and down on his line.

'Jamie, Dave, make your runs. OK, Ant, do your stuff.'

Ant picked up the ball, wiped the moisture off on his shirt and threw the ball fast and low to the near post. Jamie was there in a split second to flick it on. Dave slipped his marker and was left with the easiest of tap-ins.

'Why've you never done that before?' demanded Kev.

'Because I never come this far upfield,' said Ant. 'Unless you count corners.'

'That's right,' said Gord. 'Me and Ant are supposed to hold the line in the centre of defence. Manager's orders.'

'Well, I'm issuing new ones,' said Ronnie. 'Take up your positions again. There's no end to the lad's talent.'

Ant smiled and caught the ball from Daz's kick-out.

'Plan B, Anthony,' said Ronnie.

Ant nodded and took a short run up. This time he lofted the ball high over the defenders' heads and dropped it neatly at the far post. Dave met it and only cat-like reflexes from Daz prevented the goal.

'I never knew you could do that,' said Jimmy, admiringly.

'Neither did I,' said Jamie, 'and he's my flipping cousin.'

'Think we can use it?' asked Kev. 'A sort of secret weapon.'

'We'd be mugs not to,' said Ronnie, smoothing a hand over his rain-slicked grey hair. 'Ant could cause havoc in an unsuspecting defence. We'll use it sparingly, mind. Save it for the big occasion. Now, we've just seen what a long throw can do to your defence. Let's look at defending it.'

Only they didn't look at anything of the sort. Just at that moment Carl and Mattie put in an appearance.

'What time do you call this?' yelled Kev, marching towards them.

'Leave it out, Guv,' said Carl, backing off uneasily. 'We've had enough aggro off Brain Damage.'

'Brain Damage?'

'Yes,' said Mattie. 'Him and Costello were waiting for us by the railway bridge. They'd got the whole gang with them.'

Kev had tensed visibly. 'What did they want?'

Carl exchanged glances with Mattie. 'They wanted us to turn round and go home.'

'How come?'

'They didn't say,' Mattie answered. 'But they made it pretty clear that they didn't want us playing for the Diamonds again.'

'So that's their game,' said Kev. 'Come on, lads, let's pay them a little visit.'

'Don't you dare,' Ronnie warned. 'This is a practice session, and that's exactly what we're going to do – practise.'

'But they're trying to wreck the team,' Kev complained. 'We can't let them get away with it.'

'Leave it,' Ronnie told him. 'Carl and Mattie have shown up regardless, haven't they?'

Kev glanced at them. He didn't have much faith in either of them, and by the look on their faces, it had been a close run thing that they'd got to South Road. 'What did they say to you exactly?' he asked.

'Not much really,' Carl answered. 'Brain Damage asked if we didn't have something better to do. It wasn't so much what he said as how he said it. You know Brain Damage.'

'Oh, I know Brain Damage, all right,' said Kev. 'But it's Costello I'm more bothered about. He's one sly get. Didn't he have anything to say for himself?'

Mattie shook his head. 'He just hung round at the back.'

'That's his style,' said Kev. Costello led from the back, more a string-puller than a scrapper.

Ronnie was getting impatient. 'Come on, lads, time to get your minds back on to footy. I don't want some daft feud getting in the way of training.'

Kev wasn't finished. 'But, Ron, I just—'

'But Ron nothing. Either you get back on the field or you can spend next Sunday morning on the subs' bench. If you so much breathe on those lads, I'll relieve you of the captaincy. Do I make myself clear, Kevin?'

Kev nodded reluctantly. Threatening to make somebody else captain was a low punch.

'Good,' said Ronnie. 'Now, Gordon, can you tell me how you lost track of your man on that last throw? Nod off like that in a proper match and we could lose a vital goal.'

Kev didn't pay much attention to Gordon's mumbled excuses. His mind was elsewhere, round about the railway bridge where Carl and Mattie had been ambushed. He'd expected Costello and Brain Damage to re-surface, but not this quickly. He'd hardly had time to savour Sunday's success and he was already having to steel himself for more bother.

'Are you with us, Kevin?' shouted Ronnie.

Kev turned his head. 'Sure, I'm listening.'

But only with one ear. The west wind was booming mournfully along the Ralla, as the derelict Bootle railway line was known locally. To Kev it sounded more like the drums of war.

Six

Daft feud, is it, Ronnie? Well, tell that to Joey Bannen. The gang have been at it again, and only two days after the last time. Turning the other cheek isn't going to make them go away. Grown-ups make me sick. Like at school. Somebody takes a pop at you so you hit them back and suddenly you're the problem. Who started this war, anyway? The gang, that's who. They collared Joey outside South Parade chippy, but they picked the wrong target. Daz is the little feller's best mate and he was in the queue when Brain Damage started shoving Joey around. I'd like to have seen Brain Damage's face when Daz came storming out of the chippy. Our goalie's built like a brick wall. Only he's a wall with attitude. He doesn't lose his temper often but when he does it's a cross between Hurricane Hilda and the end of the world.

It's funny, though. I always thought Costello had more about him. He's never going to rattle the Diamonds by aggro alone. For one thing, half the Diamonds are every bit as hard as anybody in his gang. For another, even if they weren't, they're more scared of me than they are of Brain Damage! I take after my dad, you see, Tony McGovern

*Super Scally. Thanks to him, I've got the sort of reputation
a sabre toothed tiger would die for.*

*I don't feel happy about the run-in Carl and Mattie
have had with the gang, though. I get this nagging feeling
that Costello's got something else up his sleeve. I've always
thought of him as an apprentice evil genius. He's testing us,
trying to find a weak spot. Yes, that's it. He's trying to find
our weak link, our Achilles heel. You know what, quite by
accident I've just cheered myself up no end. If Costello's
looking for our weak link, he's found it at the first attempt.
I mean, Carl and Mattie aren't the most loyal characters to
pull on a Diamonds' shirt, and if* they're *not fazed by his
threats then nobody else is going to be.*

*It could just be that they're slipping. I certainly hope so.
It wouldn't half make life easier if they were.*

Seven

Mum walked across the living room and tapped Dave
on the shoulder. 'Sit down, Davey, for goodness sake.'

Dave looked round at her.

'You've got me on edge,' she explained. 'You can't
jump up every time a car goes past.'

'But he's late,' said Dave.

'Only two minutes,' said Mum, glancing at the clock.
'And that's assuming that thing's telling the right time.
It is Friday night, son. The traffic will be bad. Where's
he coming from, anyway, this George Rogan?'

'He lives off Moss Lane.'

'That's it, then,' said Mum. 'He's got to get over
Orrell Park bridge. It'll be chocker.'

Dave moved reluctantly away from the living-room
window. 'You think he's coming, though, don't you?'

'He said so on the phone, didn't he?'

'Yes.'

'So he's coming. Now just sit still and watch TV.'

Dave stared at the screen, but if you'd asked him what was on he couldn't have told you a thing. His mind was a rocket-powered camera crashing through his imagined future. Signing up for the School of Excellence, getting a YTS, signing professional forms. But they were just the boring bits, the stepping stones to glory. There was more. Making his debut at Goodison. Scoring on the volley to chalk up his first hat-trick. Hoisting some silverware above his head to the roar of the home crowd. It was only the roar of a car engine that jerked him out of his day-dream.

'Is it him?'

'Only one way to find out,' said Mum.

Dave didn't need any more encouragement. He flew to the door and wrenched it open.

'Oh, it's you.'

'Well, thank you very much,' said Dad. 'A fine welcome that was.'

'Don't tell the lad off,' said Mum. 'He's excited. He's waiting for Mr Rogan to turn up.'

'He's not here, then?'

Dave snorted. Well done, Dad. Thanks for stating the obvious.

'I'll make a cup of coffee,' said Mum.

When she came back Dave and his dad were standing side by side, peeking through the net curtains.

'Not you as well!' She said it in a mock-groan, but she was delighted to see her husband sharing Dave's excitement. 'And I thought you weren't too happy about this trial idea.'

'I wasn't at first,' said Dad.

'So what changed your mind?'

'Dunno. Seeing how much our Davey wants it, I suppose.'

Mum smiled and squeezed his arm. Normally, Dave would have cringed. He couldn't stand it when they got all lovey-dovey. But tonight he had more important things to worry about.

'Hang on,' he said. 'I think this is him.'

He watched the racing-green Toyota pull up. It was George Rogan, all right.

'Quick,' said Dad. 'Sit down. Try to look relaxed.'

'What for?'

'Don't want him thinking we're excited, do we?'

'Why not?' asked Davey.

'Bad psychology.'

'If you say so, Dad.'

The bell rang and Dave made for the front door.

'Not yet,' said Dad. 'Don't be in too much of a hurry. Play it cool. Let it ring a couple of times.'

The bell rang again. Dave moved, but Dad shook his head. At the third ring it was Mum who cracked.

'*I'll* get it.'

Dave heard Mr Rogan's voice then Mum's.

'Come into the living room.'

'Hello there, Davey lad,' said Mr Rogan breezily. 'You played well last Sunday. I can't believe the change in the Diamonds. Three months ago you were the licking boys of the whole league. Now you're half-way up the table and you've made it to the Challenge Cup final.'

'That's down to Guv,' said Dave. 'And Ronnie.'

'Don't be so modest, lad,' said Mr Rogan. 'Your goal-scoring's got a lot to do with it, too.'

Dave smiled self-consciously.

'So what's the score?' asked Dad. 'What did you want to talk to us about?'

'He's a cracking young player, your Davey,' Mr Rogan replied. 'I'd like to sign him up for four weeks. That's eight sessions. He'll be training twice a week, then we'll see what the club coaches reckon.'

'Then what?'

'A year with the School of Excellence. After that, who knows?'

'You mean you think he could make it?' asked Mum. 'As a professional footballer, I mean.'

'No promises,' said Mr Rogan. 'But he won't make it if he doesn't give it a go, will he?'

'So what does this School of Excellence involve?'

'Tell you what, come down to Bellefield and I'll show you round.'

Bellefield! Dave's heart missed a beat. 'You mean where the first team train?'

'That's right, Dave. Like the idea?'

Dave looked at Mum, then at Dad. 'Can we?'

'We're not committing ourselves to anything, are we?' asked Dad cautiously.

Mr Rogan smiled. 'Have a look round. Ask any questions. I'm sure you'll be happy with the set-up. We take care of our lads.'

Dave stared hard at Dad, willing him to say yes.

'OK,' said Dad. 'Give me the details.'

Dave couldn't restrain himself. 'Yiss! Wait till I tell the lads.'

'How will they take you quitting the Diamonds, Dave?' asked Mr Rogan.

'Quit the Diamonds! Why'd I have to do that?'

'If you join the School of Excellence, that's your football,' explained Mr Rogan. 'All of it. No Sunday League matches. You have to get a release to do that.'

'Guv will kill me.'

'I'm sure he won't,' said Mr Rogan. 'You can bet

your bottom dollar he'd take the chance with both hands.'

Dave stared at the carpet. No more Diamonds. It was unthinkable.

'You're not serious, are you, Dave?' asked Mum. 'It's only a junior league.'

Only a junior league. Since Guv appeared on the scene it had been a crusade, a holy war.

'It's your decision, son,' said Dad.

Dave thought of Goodison and the stepping stones to glory.

'It's all right,' he said. 'I'll give it a go.'

Eight

'Penny for them, Dave.'

It was Kev.

'What's that, Guv?'

'Your thoughts. A penny for them. You were miles away.'

Dave continued lacing his boots. 'I don't know what I was thinking. My mind just goes blank sometimes.'

It wasn't true. Since George Rogan's bombshell about giving up the Diamonds, he'd only had one thing on his mind – how to break the news to his mates. It was like every time one of them came near him he heard this little voice in his head: *Traitor, Turncoat.*

'Ant's mind is always blank,' chuckled Kev. 'Isn't that right?'

Ant shook his head and pulled on his shirt. 'We'd better get moving,' he said. 'Fix-It are already out there.'

'Keen, eh?' said Jamie. 'We'll put a stop to that.'

Dave stood up and jogged on the spot for a few seconds. 'All right,' he announced. 'I'm ready.'

And there it was again. That voice. *Traitor, Turncoat.*

'Right, lads,' said Kev. 'This is the captain of your ship. Orders of the day. Three points. Nothing else will do.'

The other boys nodded.

'OK, let's go for it.'

The Diamonds took the field to the strains of the Rocky theme, courtesy of Ratso's ghetto blaster.

'Turn it up, Mike,' shouted Ratso. 'It's meant to psych the opposition. Give it the bifters.'

Mike Mintoe, who was cradling the huge ghetto blaster, winked and turned it up to full volume. 'I hope this isn't for long, Rats,' he said, 'or I'll have burst eardrums on top of everything else.'

Dave frowned and wondered how Mike could be so cheerful when he was stuck in a wheelchair for the rest of his life. He wondered how he would react if anything like that happened to him.

'Hey, Dave,' shouted Kev. 'Snap out of it.'

Dave cast his eyes over the opposition. Fix-It were a decent mid-table outfit, but he was confident that on recent form the Diamonds would dispatch them without much difficulty.

Kev won the toss. 'Our kick-off,' he declared.

Dave nodded. At the whistle he rolled the ball to Jamie and received it back. Blocked by a couple of eager-beaver central defenders he turned and found Ratso with a short pass. Ratso knocked it out to Bashir on the wing and Dave started his run forward.

'Bash, Bash!' he shouted, arm raised, but Bashir passed him over in favour of John racing down the right. The cross-field ball wrong-footed the Fix-It defence and John put Jamie through on goal. Jamie struck it hard and low across the box and Kev was only inches from connecting.

'Good movement,' Ronnie shouted encouragingly from the touch-line. 'Keep it up.'

Gord broke up the Fix-It attack and punted the ball to Jimmy. A nifty one-two with Bashir put Jimmy clear just outside the penalty area.

'My ball,' Dave shouted.

But again he was ignored. This time Jimmy favoured Joey making a forward run from defence. Controlling it skilfully, Joey struck a high cross to the far post. The Fix-It goalie could only flap at it like a short-sighted parrot, leaving Jamie with the sort of simple finish it would be criminal to pass up. He met it with a powerful header.

One-nil.

It made no sense, but Dave couldn't help wondering: did somebody know something already? Did they know he was planning to bail out? Is that why he was being left out all of a sudden? Then he dismissed the idea. It was just paranoia. No, the lads trusted him, and that made him feel even worse.

Traitor, Turncoat.

As Dave strolled back to the centre circle generously applauding the goal he noticed George Rogan. He gave him a nod of greeting then glanced round at his team-mates. He was feeling horribly guilty. After a spell of pressure by Fix-It, the Diamonds came back strongly. Dave had started to come into the game more, but he still hadn't found his range. That all changed with a pass to his feet by Bashir. Dave turned his marker and ran on strongly into the penalty area. The Fix-It keeper was off his line like a greyhound, but Dave was ready for him. Jinking to the left he beat the goalie with a clinical chip.

Two-nil.

George Rogan gave him the thumbs up. Dave smiled an embarrassed smile. Leave it out, he thought, the other lads would be bound to know something was going on.

Five minutes later, the Diamonds went three up. This time Dave turned provider, beating his man with a neat nutmeg out on the touch-line. Reaching the goal-line he struck the ball hard and low across the goalmouth. Kev met it with his chest.

Three-nil at half-time.

The Diamonds were all set for more of the same in the second half when Costello's gang arrived.

'Terrific,' murmured Kev. 'I wondered when they'd turn up.'

'Ignore them,' said Dave. 'Once they find out we're three-nil up, they'll soon lose interest.'

They didn't. They jeered and hooted, and did their best to put the Diamonds off. All except Costello. He just stared at Kev, trying to psych him out.

'Forget Costello,' Dave insisted, sensing Kev's anger building. 'Let's enjoy ourselves.'

It had been the theme of Ronnie's half-time pep-talk only he had used a bit of classic manager-speak: express yourselves. Unfortunately, it wasn't the Diamonds who started to express themselves. Maybe they were rattled by the catcalls from Costello's gang, maybe they were over-confident after their first-half display, maybe they'd just lost concentration after the break. Whatever the reason, they found themselves on the back foot with Fix-It flying at them.

'Gord!' Kev yelled. 'You're too wide. Look at the space between you and Ant.'

'Too wide, eh, McGovern?' Brain Damage mimicked sarcastically. 'Bit like the empty space between your ears.'

Kev shot a hostile glance at his long-time enemy.

'Don't you go walkabout, too,' shouted Dave. 'Get your mind on the game, Guv. They're taking us to the cleaners.'

As if to prove the point, one of the Fix-It midfielders ran powerfully through the middle of the Diamonds' defence, laid the ball off and took the return pass on the edge of the penalty area. Rushing out bravely, Daz managed to smother the pass, but it was struck with real venom and ran clear. The tall Fix-It striker was left with a simple tap-in.

Three-one.

'Wake up,' bawled Daz. 'You left me completely exposed then. Where was my flipping cover? What do you think you were playing at, Gord? As for you, Guv, you just stood there like a rotten space cadet and let that lad go straight past you. Forgotten how to tackle, have you? Gone tackle-ophobic?'

'Shut it, Daz,' snapped Kev. 'You're the one who didn't hold the shot.'

Everybody on the field knew that was a cheap dig. An unfair one, too. Daz had done brilliantly to beat it out at all. Ronnie was pacing the touch-line. If there was something he could do without, then it was one of the famous Diamond tantrums.

'Come off it, Guv,' said Dave. 'It wasn't Daz's fault. We went to sleep, all of us.'

But the *us* stuck in his throat. He was almost an outsider already.

Traitor, Turncoat.

Bashir on the wing found himself as affected by the Diamonds' sudden spell of the jitters as his defence. He accidentally trod on the ball as he ran and tumbled over in mid-flight, much to the pleasure of Costello and Co. There weren't too many black kids on the Diamond, so Bashir had to take a lot of aggro. He rose unsteadily to his feet with the ugly sound of monkey noises in his ears. As if to rub salt in his wounds, Fix-It had ripped the Diamonds' defence wide-open with a quick-fire counter attack. Ant blocked one shot with a desperate lunge, but Fix-It put the ball in the net with a terrific volley from the rebound.

Three-two

Suddenly the confident swagger with which the Diamonds had left the field at half-time was replaced with anxious glances and squabbling. They could actually feel Fix-It breathing down their necks. An equalizer seemed inevitable.

'For crying out loud, Bash,' groaned Joey. 'You can't lose the ball in that sort of position.'

'He didn't do it on purpose,' Dave shot back.

'So? He did it, didn't he?'

Bashir simply stood crestfallen. It was bad enough taking abuse off Costello's gang. He hadn't expected it from his team-mates.

Costello leant over to Brain Damage. 'Listen to them,' he said. 'Can't take it when the chips are down, can they?'

Kev turned and made for the hecklers. Seeing the danger signs, Dave raced across to restrain him. 'Behave, Guv,' he said. 'That's exactly what they want you to do. You've already had one suspension this year.'

Jamie and Ratso were on hand to back him up.

'He's right,' said Ratso. 'Another punch-up and you're out of the final.'

Kev stiffened, remembering the way he'd had to sit out the semi-final on the touch-line.

'Come on, Guv,' said Jamie. 'We're still three-two up. All we've got to do is play ourselves back into it. Don't let those morons get to you.'

Kev nodded and turned away. Brain Damage and Costello responded with loud chicken noises.

'I know, I know,' Kev hissed as all eyes turned towards him, 'I'll ignore them.'

He winced as he realised how close he'd come to losing it. His raging bull act was just what the gang wanted.

For the next ten minutes Fix-It continued to press. Twice they brought spectacular saves out of Daz when they were through on goal. The second, an athletic tip-over, led to a corner.

'Come on, lads,' shouted Kev. 'We've got to defend this.'

The Diamonds had got the message. They had all ten outfield players back. It was a good corner, clearing the near post and swinging in, just out of Daz's reach. A Fix-It forward met it with a wicked glancing header, but Dave was covering the back post. His solid header cleared the penalty area, wrong-footing the attacking side. Suddenly it was a race between Bashir and two Fix-It players to reach the loose ball. It was no contest. The Diamonds' Somali winger was a thunderbolt on legs. He dropped his shoulder to lose the two possible markers, pushed it wide, turned and set off downfield. Dave was already flying out of defence to give him support.

'Bash,' he yelled as he caught up with play. 'Square ball.'

Bashir nodded and put Dave clear. He steadied himself and looked up. In two minds whether to come or not, the goalie was off his line. With hardly any backlift, Dave lofted a perfectly-weighted chip over the keeper's head. As the ball nestled in the Fix-It goal, Bashir gave the gang a cool stare. *Call me monkey now*, he was challenging them.

'Four-two', said Kev with obvious satisfaction. 'Now let's sew it up.' He knew that Bash and Dave had just conjured up the goal that killed the game. Fix-It had looked on the verge of an equalizer, but the Diamonds' lightning break had restored their two-goal cushion. There was no way back for Fix-It. Brain Damage and Costello had also reconciled themselves to a Diamonds' victory and slunk away quietly.

'That was brilliant, Dave,' Kev enthused. 'What'd we do without you?'

Dave gave him a strained smile. 'I couldn't have done it without Bash.' Once more he heard the voice. *Traitor, Turncoat.*

In the last five minutes the Diamonds turned the screw on their demoralized opponents. The Fix-It defenders were being pulled all over the field as Bashir, Jamie and Dave knocked the ball around confidently and Kev and John raided from midfield. It was an exhibition match from then on. Kev and Jamie each scored from distance and Dave chalked up his hat-trick with a diving header in stoppage time.

'Dave,' Kev called as the final whistle blew. 'This is yours, I reckon.' He threw him the match ball. 'Nice one.'

Dave smiled as he caught the ball, but he felt awful. Really bad.

'You're going to be a tough act to follow,' said Kev.

A heart-string tugged. 'I beg your pardon?'

'When you sign for the School of Excellence,' Kev explained.

Dave just stared at him, lost for words.

'That's right, isn't it, Ratso?' Kev asked the Diamonds' very own walking encyclopaedia. 'You do have to drop out of Sunday football when you're picked for the School of Excellence, don't you?'

Ratso shrugged nonchalantly. 'As far as I know.'

Dave couldn't believe his ears. They'd known all along!

'Anyway,' said Kev. 'Let us know when it's your last game and we'll try to make it a bit special. From all the lads ...' Kev seemed genuinely moved. 'Best of luck, Davey lad.'

'Yes, ta, Guv.'

Dave knew it was a lame reply, but it was the best he could manage. It was moments like that when he realized why they'd chosen Kev to skipper the side. He stood and watched the rest of the team jogging towards the changing-rooms. Ant was complaining that he hadn't been allowed to try his long throw. Ratso was arguing with Gord over a point of football history. They'd lost their star striker and were just carrying on regardless. These Diamonds, they were truly amazing.

Nine

Funny how this season's turned out. When I joined the Diamonds they were propping up the table. Lousy morale and a worse manager. Then it all started to turn around. We got shot of old Bobby Jones – that's right, Gord's dad – and Ronnie took over as coach. Then I taught the lads how to scrap for every ball, how to believe in themselves.

Suddenly anything was possible. Now we're in the final with only Longmoor Celtic between ourselves and the trophy, and what happens? Our best player gets talent-spotted. Oh, I put a brave face on it at the match this morning, but I don't feel too brilliant about it. I mean, Dave's got class. We can really have our backs to the wall and he'll turn a hopeful punt upfield into a goal. He's a predator. He's got the instincts of an assassin, always knows where the goal is and is quick enough with his feet to convert the hardest of half-chances. So it's a bit of a sickener that we're going to lose him a few weeks before the Challenge Cup final. It's probably killed our chances of winning a trophy this season. Jamie's the only natural striker left in the squad and it's too late to register anybody new.

Mind you, there's a silver lining to every cloud. At least we seem to have shut Costello and Brain Damage up. They did their best to put us off our game, but our seven goals silenced them. It was only after I'd congratulated Dave on his trial (pretty big of me, don't you think?) that I noticed they'd gone, so I suppose we can get down to the business of finding a new formation without distractions.

And let's face it, without Davey Lafferty up front, we're going to need all the help we can get.

Ten

Ding ding ding.

Dave was home from the victory over Fix-It.

Woof woof woof.

Dixie was waiting.

'Oh, not again,' came Mum's voice from indoors. 'Dave and that stupid doorbell.'

But this is important.

Ding ding ding.

Woof woof woof.

'Do you have to ring like that?' shouted Mum. 'I'm not deaf, you know.'

Dave peered through the frosted glass of the door. He could see her coming, but it didn't stop him ringing.

Of course I have to ring like this. I've got some news. Hurry up.

Ding ding ding.

Woof woof woof.

Mum's voice: 'Just wait, will you? I'm coming as quickly as I can. Dixie, get down.'

Dad's voice: 'Get your hand off that bell.'

Dixie's voice: *Woof woof WO-OOF!*

Finally Mum opened it. 'You'll have this broken, you will. And look what you made me do.'

Dixie was licking his paw.

'I fell over your braindead mutt of a dog. What's all the commotion this time?'

'Mum, I saw ...'

But Dad arrived as he was about to tell his news.

'You know what we ought to call you?' he said. 'Quasi-flipping-modo. You're that mad about bells. We ought to get you your own belfry. Yes, maybe that's what you'll be when you grow up, the guardian of one of the cathedrals in town. The Hunchback of Paddy's Wigwam.'

Paddy's Wigwam was the Metropolitan Cathedral, a building that looked more like a spaceship than a church.

'Look at it,' Dad went on. 'You'll have that doorbell worn away. Bell erosion, that's what we'll have.'

Dave rolled his eyes. Yes, and he'd have ear erosion.

What was it about dads that made them do a joke to death?

'The bells,' Dad continued, doing his Quasimodo impression, capering down the hallway.

'Da-ad,' groaned Dave. 'Somebody will see you.'

'Davey's right,' said Mum. 'You're making a show of yourself. Thirty-three going on four years old, that's you. Act your age.'

Dad grabbed her hands and started waltzing her into the living room. 'Esmerelda,' he drooled. 'My Esmerel-da.'

'Oh, get off,' said Mum. She was trying to sound angry, but it came out giggly.

Dave shook his head and shut the door. Why can't parents act their age? They can be such an embarrassment sometimes.

'Anyway,' said Mum, disentangling herself from Dad. 'You were telling me something before we were so rudely interrupted.'

Dad gave a mischievous grin and settled down to read the Sunday paper.

Dave sat in an armchair and scratched behind Dixie's ear to keep him quiet. 'We won,' he said. 'Seven-two. I got a hat-trick.'

Mum was about to interrupt, but Dave was on a roll.

'But that isn't half of it. Mr Rogan was at the game.'

Dad lowered his paper.

'He wants to know if we want to go round Bellefield tomorrow.'

'Tomorrow,' said Mum. 'But won't that clash with training with the Diamonds?'

Dave threw back his head. 'Oh heck. I forgot.'

'*You*,' said Dad, 'forgetting the Diamonds. Now there's a novelty.'

'I was so excited about Bellefield,' said Dave. 'I couldn't think about anything else.'

'Does it matter?' asked Dad. 'You're giving up soon, anyway.'

'I know,' said Dave, 'Maybe it isn't such a disaster. The Diamonds know I'm leaving.'

'You told them?'

'No, they already knew. Besides, Mr Rogan wants us at Bellefield straight after school. I can probably get to South Road for the last half hour. I'll be able to put in an appearance, at least.'

'Straight after school, you say?' asked Dad. 'That'll mean me asking for half an hour off work.'

'I could always take him,' said Mum. 'You could follow us up there.'

'No,' Dad replied. 'I want to be there for all of it. I'm sure it'll be OK with the boss. Even our management is football crazy. Old man Sedgefield's got a season ticket for Anfield.'

'Wrong side of Stanley Park,' said Dave with a disapproving frown.

'I quite agree,' said Dad. 'But he'll let me off early for something like this, and that's all that matters.'

Mum smiled. She was relieved to see him showing interest in Dave's ambitions.

'Excited, son?'

'Not half,' Dave answered. 'I won't sleep a wink.'

'You better had,' said Dad. 'You've still got school, remember.'

Not for the first time, Dave rolled his eyes. Lighten up, Dad, he thought.

'Anyway,' said Dad. 'That's enough about football ...'

'Thank goodness for that,' said Mum.

'Let's have a video instead,' said Dad winking at Dave.

Dave watched him take the video off the shelf. Everton's 1995 FA Cup win over Manchester United.

'Oh, give me strength,' said Mum, only half-seriously.

Dad chuckled and tossed a cushion at her as she walked out.

Dave smiled. Life had never been better.

Eleven

'I'm not late, am I?' asked Dad, climbing off his bike.

'No,' said Dave, his heart dropping suddenly into his feet. 'But I didn't think you'd come like that.'

Dad looked down at his jet black, skin-tight cycling gear. 'What's wrong with me?'

Dave shook his head. 'If you don't see it, I can't tell you.'

Dad followed Mum and Dave into Everton's training-ground. 'But what is it? So I'm wearing my cycling suit. What's the big deal?'

'At least take off the wimpy helmet,' hissed Dave as George Rogan stepped forward to greet them.

Dad did as he was told. He was about to ask for the third time what was wrong with wearing his cycling gear, but Mum silenced him with a warning look.

'Are any of the players here?' asked Dave.

'Sorry, son,' said George. 'They knocked off at noon.'

'Oh.' Dave felt a twinge of disappointment, but it was only a twinge. He was, after all, going to be taken on a guided tour of a Premiership training-ground.

'Would you like a cup of tea, Mr and Mrs Lafferty?' asked George.

'Wouldn't say no,' said Dad.

Holding their mugs of tea, the Laffertys were soon following George around Bellefield.

'These are the changing-rooms,' said George, pushing open the door.

'Pooh,' said Mum, wrinkling her nose.

'Yes,' said George with a rueful smile, 'it does get a bit whiffy, doesn't it?'

'Our Dave will feel at home,' said Dad, tousling his hair. 'You need a gas mask to enter his room.'

Dave winced. First the cycle suit, now this. Dad couldn't be more embarrassing if he tried.

'Sauna,' said George. 'Showers, baths, and in here … the kit room.'

Dave looked at the rows of boots and remembered what Ratso had told him. If he did get a YTS with Everton, he'd probably end up cleaning and polishing that lot. Beside him, Mum's face was all puckered. She definitely did not like the smell of sweaty feet.

'You could do with air-conditioning,' she said.

George just smiled. 'Is that a camera?' he asked, pointing to her open shoulder-bag.

'Yes, would you mind?'

'Of course not,' said George. 'In fact,' he reached up to a peg on the wall, 'why not snap Dave wearing this?'

Dave registered the initials HK on the coat. It belonged to the club manager. 'You sure?'

'Sure I'm sure,' said George. 'Slip it on.'

Dave's hands didn't reach half-way down the sleeves. He knew he must look stupid but it didn't matter. He just couldn't stop smiling.

'Say cheese,' George told him.

'Cheese.'

'And one with Mum and Dad?'

Dave took a look at Dad's ridiculous outfit and started to shake his head, but his parents were already in position, posing with their arms round his shoulder.

'That's one for the family album,' said George.

Over my dead body, thought Dave.

'Now to the business end,' said George. 'Have you given any more thought to Dave signing forms, Mr and Mrs Lafferty?'

'You mean now?'

'If you wish,' said George. 'I'll introduce you to the Youth Development Officer. It's up to you. There's no rush. Give it a bit more thought if you like.'

Dave looked up hopefully. He was inspecting Dad's face. Mum's support was already in the bag.

'Why not?' said Dad. 'If this is what you really want, son.'

Dave nodded vigorously. 'It is.'

They climbed the stairs and went into an office. Moments later Dave was giving his details. Date of birth, age, school. Then, with a shaking hand, he was signing a form in four copies. One for himself, one for his school, one for the club and one for the FA.

'Your lad is a good player,' said George, as he led the Laffertys downstairs, 'but there's loads of competition. You know what my job is now?'

Shakes of the head all round.

'I've got to find somebody better.'

Dave just stared at him.

'Sounds hard, doesn't it, lad?'

Dave nodded.

'Well, that's the way it is. Only the best of the best get through. My job as a scout is to spot them and sign them for Everton. I hope you're the one, Dave, the lad who's got the vision, the determination and the skill to make it. It's up to you now.'

'I can do it,' Dave replied firmly. 'I know I can.'

'We might as well go home now,' grumbled Brain Damage.

'Stop moaning,' said Costello, walking along the crumbling wall opposite South Road Community Centre.

'But they took no notice of us,' said Brain Damage. It had really got under his skin. McGovern had been ready for them. He'd got the Diamonds together somewhere and had led them in together for the training session.

'I'm thinking,' said Costello.

'A lot of good that's done us,' said Brain Damage. 'You said we were going to break up the Diamonds. Look at them.' He pointed to the boys jogging round the Community Centre field. They were laughing and joking as they went through their paces.

'I'll come up with something,' said Costello. 'You see if I don't.'

Brain Damage could hear Kev exchanging banter with Bashir and Jamie. He was seething inside. Two weeks they'd been trying to sabotage the Diamonds and what did they have to show for it? A seven-two victory for the enemy and a load of frustration for them.

'Well, you'd better do it quick,' said Brain Damage. 'Just listen to them, will you? They're laughing at us.'

Costello was running his eyes over the squad as they broke up into passing groups. 'I'm sure there's some-body missing, you know.'

'Big deal.'

'No, it could be important.'

'OK, so there's somebody missing. Who?'

'Tez,' said Costello. 'I bet you never got that list of players I asked for.'

'I did, you know,' said Tez.

'Well done,' said Costello. 'I'm impressed.'

Tez beamed. He'd passed his test. Brain Damage scowled. Whose mate was he anyway?

Costello ran his eyes down the page, then tapped the paper with his forefinger. 'Lafferty,' he said. 'He isn't here.'

'Maybe he's injured,' said Brain Damage.

'Maybe,' said Costello. 'I hope so. They'd certainly miss him against Longmoor.'

'Hang on,' said Tez. 'Isn't that him getting out of that car?'

Costello and Brain Damage saw Dave jump out of his parents' car at the top of the road and wave as they drove off.

'I don't believe it,' Costello gloated. 'This is too good to be true.'

The rest of the gang stared at Costello, waiting for an explanation. 'We've been doing it all wrong,' he said. 'We've been trying to find the weak link. Well, I've got a better idea. Who scores all their goals?'

Brain Damage followed the direction of Costello's eyes. 'Lafferty.'

'Exactly,' said Costello. 'It isn't the weak link we're going to break, it's the strong one.'

Checking that nobody on the field was watching, Costello led the gang to intercept Dave.

'Get out of my way,' said Dave. 'What do you want, anyway?'

Costello nudged Brain Damage.

'You and me,' said Brain Damage by way of a challenge. 'Mano a mano.'

— 47 —

It was something he'd heard in an American gangster movie. It had sounded really cool, but Dave simply laughed. 'Behave,' he said. 'The rest of your mates will just jump me.'

'No way,' said Brain Damage. 'Me and you.'

'If you can beat Andy,' Costello said, 'we'll leave the Diamonds alone for good.'

Usually Dave would have carried on walking, but he was fired up after his visit to Bellefield. He was a star. Nothing could touch him.

'All right,' he said. 'But I'm going to whip you, lad.'

'Not if I whip you first,' said Brain Damage, throwing himself at Dave.

Dave sprang back and struck his attacker on the cheek. Brain Damage touched his face then charged Dave again, making him topple over the low roadside wall.

'Get him, Andy,' shouted the gang members. 'Smash his face in.'

But Dave was already fighting back. He rolled over and pinned Brain Damage's arms with his knees.

'Give up, Brain Damage,' he said, 'or I'll make that ugly gob of yours even uglier.'

'Get off me!' roared Brain Damage, twisting and struggling.

'Make me.'

Dave was on top and that was how he planned to stay.

'Get off!' Brain Damage repeated.

'Give up, Brain Damage,' said Dave. 'Just—'

He didn't finish the sentence. Something was happening to him. First it was pins and needles in his right hand, then in his arm, his shoulder, his face. Then a taste in the back of his throat accompanied by a strange smell, strong and choking. Brain Damage took advantage of his opponent's distraction and tugged his arm free.

Dave wasn't even aware of the fist coming at him, or of the shouts of his team-mates suddenly alerted to the fight. He was out of it. The shouts were a dull boom, Brain Damage's punches a vague pressure a long way away. Everything was swallowed up in the overwhelming rush of panic. It was like everything was coming at him. Brain Damage's punches rocked Dave back but he didn't even feel it. Just the taste and the smell and the wave of panic.

'You've got him!' Costello yelled in delight. 'Finish it, Andy.'

Brain Damage rolled Dave over and started smashing his fist into his face. Once, twice, three times.

'Ugh,' said Tez. 'Look at him. He's slobbering.'

'Foaming at the mouth, you mean,' said Costello, leaning forward.

'What's the matter with him?' Brain Damage exclaimed, starting back in horror. 'He's shaking.'

'I don't like it,' said Tez. 'He looks weird.'

But the moment passed. Thanks to Costello. 'He's just got the shakes,' he announced. 'Must be petrified. You've done him good style, Andy.'

Brain Damage looked down doubtfully at his victim. 'I think there's something wrong. What's the matter with him?'

Costello rolled his eyes. 'Don't tell me you're going to go easy on him,' he said, 'just because he's acting funny.'

Grimacing at Dave's jerking body, Brain Damage hit him once more for good luck, before raising his arms in victory.

'Come on, Andy,' said Costello. 'I think the divvy's

got the message. You have, haven't you, Lafferty? Play for the Diamonds and that's what you're going to get. Isn't that right, lads?'

There was a loud cheer, followed by the chant of: 'One Andy Ramage, there's only one Andy Ramage.'

Kev and Jamie were the first of the Diamonds to arrive.

'What have you done, Brain Damage?' yelled Kev.

'I took him,' he gloated. 'It was easy. I'll take you next, McGovern, just you wait and see.'

'He's really hurt,' said Jamie, leaning over Dave.

But as they walked away in triumph the gang weren't aware of what the Diamonds saw – the final few rhythmic jerking movements of Dave's body or the blueish tinge round his lips and mouth. They didn't see that, long after the beating, he lay very still on the ground.

Twelve

I'm scared, really scared. I've seen fights before, lots of them, but I've never seen anybody get in the state Dave was in today. He was shaking all over and there was white stuff on his mouth. Then he just seemed to go to sleep. John said he was dead. We told O'Hara to keep his stupid mouth shut. It was Ronnie who got a grip of things. He put Dave in the recovery position and sent Jimmy to his mum's to phone for an ambulance. Jimmy only lives round the corner from the Community Centre.

Everybody was dead quiet while we waited. After a couple of minutes Dave came to, but he was confused and really tired. None of us could figure it. He should have been able to handle Brain Damage, but he was completely out of it. All of a sudden everybody became an expert.

Daz: It must have been a blow to the head.

John: Brain Damage put a hex on Dave. (Trust O'Hara to come up with something stupid.)

Ant: His brain had got over-excited on account of the visit to Bellefield. (I told Ant his brain would never get over-excited.)

It was Ratso who came up with a better idea. Dave had had a fit. We were still mulling this over, wondering what it meant, when we heard the ambulance siren. Gord and Ratso ran into the road waving their arms. That's when it got scary. I mean, I thought they'd maybe give Dave a pill or something, then he'd be right as rain. Dave's dead fit. He couldn't have anything seriously wrong with him. But the ambulance people decided to take him away. They wouldn't even let him walk to the ambulance. They put him in a wheelchair like the one Mike has. And there were all these questions. How old was he? Had it ever happened before? Could somebody contact his parents? Then he was gone.

We all just stood there, watching the ambulance speeding across the estate. Then Ratso said what we'd all been thinking. We'd all been so jealous of Dave because of the Everton trial, but who'd want to be in his shoes now?

PART TWO

An Injury to All

One

Dave turned round at the sound of his cubicle curtains being drawn back. It was his parents.

Mum was the first to speak. 'Davey, are you all right?'

Dave looked into her face, then at Dad hovering a little behind her and to her left. They both looked ill-at-ease in the crowded casualty unit.

'What happened, son?'

'Dunno.'

'But what did the doctor say?'

'Nothing.'

'He must have said something,' said Dad, clearly irritated at the reluctant reply.

'He asked me some questions.'

Dave wasn't in the mood for the third degree. He was dazed and tired and he felt a bit embarrassed, but most of all he was bored. OK, he'd had a funny turn. So what? Why wouldn't they just let him go home? He'd already decided that he hated hospitals. It was the way nothing ever seemed to happen. Some questions, then ages while you lay on your back and stared up at the ceiling or rolled on to your side and counted the floor tiles. More questions or maybe a nurse poking her head round the corner asking if you were all right – which you weren't, of course – then nothing.

Mum wasn't about to let it go. 'Mr Mintoe said you'd been in a fight. Took a blow to the head, or something.'

Dave kept his eyes fixed stubbornly on a dog-eared poster on the far wall. 'I don't remember.'

'Then try,' said Dad, impatience creeping into his voice. 'Ronnie said it was that Andrew Ramage. He had something to do with this.'

'Sort of.'

'What do you mean "sort of"? Either he did or he didn't.'

'I can't remember, OK? I can't naffing remember.' Dave almost shouted. It was bad enough trying to sort things out in his own head, never mind make somebody else understand what had happened to him. For some unknown reason he started to cry.

'Take your time, son,' Mum said, putting her arm round his shoulders. 'We won't put any pressure on you.'

Dave glimpsed Mum mouthing something to Dad. He was glad of her protection from the old man's interrogation. Dad was always like this when something went wrong. If you hurt yourself he would start shouting – like it was your fault. Just his way, Dave thought, but really annoying. He leaned his head wearily against Mum.

'There was a fight,' he said. 'But I don't think that started it. I came over all funny. I can't explain it really. It just happened.'

'But you did have a fight?' asked Dad. 'This Ramage boy hurt you?'

'No, I was winning. I had him down with his shoulders pinned. He didn't touch me. Then I went sort of dizzy, tingly.' Dave's voice trailed off. 'I got this funny taste in my mouth. Oh, I don't know.'

Again, it was Mum who tried to comfort him. 'It's all right, Davey. Just rest for a moment or two.'

Once again, Dave was aware of the looks passing between his parents. It was weird. He'd been upset before they arrived, angry that Brain Damage might think he'd actually got the better of him, but not really scared. Now that was changing. It was the fear in their voices. *They* were scaring him.

'Am I ill?' he asked.

'We don't know anything yet,' said Mum, unable to hide the tremor in her voice.

'You read about things,' said Dave, his anxiety mounting. 'Growths. On your brain. What's the word?'

'It won't be anything serious,' Mum told him. She said it quickly. Rather too quickly. Like she didn't want the thought to even enter his mind. Her attempt at reassurance actually made things worse.

'It was probably just a faint,' said Dad, not too convincingly. 'Your mum used to faint when we first got married.' A little chuckle entered his voice. 'She passed out on the loo once.'

Dave allowed himself to be side-tracked. 'She never!'

'She did. I had to run in and hold her upright.'

'Thank you very much,' said Mum, only half-seriously. 'I really need you broadcasting that particular story.'

Dave found himself smiling, then wondered what he had to smile about and lay back on his pillows. 'I wonder when they're going to let me go home.'

'We should know in a minute,' said Dad. 'Here's the doctor.'

'Mr and Mrs Lafferty?' he enquired.

Dave's parents nodded in unison.

'I'm Dr Choudhury. I've examined David and taken his blood pressure.'

'And?'

'Will he be all right?'

'I don't want you to worry,' said Dr Choudhury. 'David seems to have recovered well, but I'd like you to make an appointment so we can take another look at him. We need to do some tests.'

Dave listened to them and wondered when somebody was going to say something to him.

After all, it was his brain they were talking about.

'What sort of tests?'

'I want you to make an appointment for a CT scan.'

'What's that?'

'You may have heard it called a brain scan.'

'Oh no!' At his mother's cry, Dave felt like dying. Now he knew the score. It *was* serious.

'Please don't worry, Mrs Lafferty,' said Dr Choudhury. 'It's simply a harmless and painless way to produce pictures of the brain. We need to determine what's going on.'

'It doesn't mean ...?'

Great. She'd been the one who'd been telling him not to panic. So what does *she* do?

'It doesn't mean anything, Mrs Lafferty. It's a matter of making an accurate diagnosis.'

'So what does it do, this CT scan?' asked Dad.

'The machine uses X-rays to produce images of the brain. They're then fed into a computer.'

'And that will tell you what's wrong?'

'It may.'

Mum frowned. Dad tugged nervously at his ear lobe.

'There is another test.'

'We're listening.'

'An EEG, or electroencephalogram.'

'Come again?'

'A what-o-whatagram?'

'It is a bit of a mouthful, isn't it?' said Doctor Choudhury with a smile. 'We attach some electrodes to David's head ...' He glanced down. 'It doesn't hurt.'

At last, thought Dave, somebody had actually remembered he was there, listening to them.

'Then the EEG machine records and measures the tiny electrical signals produced inside the brain. You may have heard them referred to as brainwaves.'

Mum leaned forward. 'There are no side effects, are there?'

'None at all. It's all routine and harmless, but it will give us the information we need to treat David correctly.'

Dave listened to the verbal ping-pong passing overhead and suddenly sat bolt upright. 'What about the trial?' he asked.

'Trial?' asked Dr Choudhury.

'For Everton. My School of Excellence.'

Dr Choudhury looked to Mum and Dad for an explanation.

'Football,' said Dad simply.

'It may be wise to wait for the results before you undertake any strenuous exercise,' said Dr Choudhury.

'Wait?' cried Dave. 'I can't wait.'

'Well, you'll just have to,' said Mum. 'This is your health we're talking about.'

'But I'm all right,' Dave protested. 'There's nothing wrong with me.'

'Just be patient,' said Dr Choudhury. 'Once we know what's happening in here ...' he tapped Dave's forehead gently with his forefinger, '... you'll probably be able to carry on with your football career. Like Arthur Shearer.'

There was a moment's shocked silence. Like he'd said the Pope went bungee-jumping.

'Have I said something wrong?'

'Sort of,' said Dad. 'For a start, it's Alan, Alan Shearer.'

'Oh.'

'And he's a Newcastle United player.'

'Is that bad?'

Dad smiled. 'Round here it is.'

Dave stared at the ceiling. Thanks to his stupid brain, he wasn't going to be any sort of footballer, not even an Arthur Shearer.

Two

'Do you think we should keep him off school?' Mum wondered aloud as she walked into the kitchen. 'It is Friday. One day wouldn't make much difference.' She was bundling yesterday's papers into a bin-bag while Dad got his packed lunch out of the fridge.

'I am here, you know,' Dave protested. He had his mouth full of cereal and started spraying soggy Frosties all over the table. 'And I don't want to stay off. I'm bored stiff sitting round the house. You've had me dossing here for nearly a week.'

At the sound of his voice, Mum and Dad turned and stared at him, as if they'd forgotten he had the power of speech. It had started at the hospital, this talking about him as if he wasn't there. To begin with it had been annoying. Now it was really doing his head in.

'You can't be too careful,' said Mum, running the dish cloth over the table in front of Dave.

'You can, you know,' said Dad. 'I know it's scary, the way he blacked out but it doesn't mean we have to feather-bed him all the time.'

Dave found himself nodding. To listen to Mum, you'd think he'd broken his leg or lost an eye, or something.

Unfortunately, Mum wasn't having any. 'Typical man!' she snapped. 'If there's a problem you just shut your eyes and hope it goes away.'

Dave's head sagged. Not again. It had been like this ever since his black-out. Squabble, squabble, squabble. The Lafferty household had always been completely the opposite until now. Since his funny turn life had gone right downhill.

'I'm not doing anything of the sort,' Dad retorted. 'All I'm saying is, we should try to carry on as normal—'

'What's just happened to Davey isn't normal,' Mum interrupted. 'What if it happens again?'

Dad glanced at the kitchen clock. 'Look, we'll have to discuss this tonight.' He picked up the holdall he always took to work. 'I'm going to be late.'

'That's it,' snapped Mum. 'Run off to work like nothing's happened.'

Dad sighed and put the holdall on the worktop near the sink. 'Well, I'm certainly not going out while you're in this mood. Come on, spit it out. What do you want me to say?'

Mum started rattling the dishes in the sink. Not washing them, *rattling* them. Earthquake Lafferty had struck. Dave was glad he wasn't a cup.

'Talk to me, will you?' seethed Dad.

Dave laid his arms on the table and made a nest for his head. This was all his fault. Why did he have to get into a fight with Brain Damage in the first place?

'I just want you to back me over this,' said Mum. 'You're acting as if nothing has happened. Our son has only just got out of hospital.'

'I know very well where he was,' Dad answered hotly. 'I was there with you, remember. He isn't just your son.'

'He is when there's a problem,' said Mum acidly.

'Now that's not fair,' Dad protested.

Mum didn't meet his eyes.

'They're going to do tests, aren't they?' Dad continued. 'I don't see why we can't just get on with our lives till then.'

'But what if …?' Mum hesitated.

'What if what?' asked Dad.

'Davey love,' said Mum. 'Pop in the living room, will you?'

'Why?'

'Because I asked you to.'

'You're going to talk about me, aren't you?' he asked.

'Do as your mum says, Dave,' Dad told him.

'But it's about me,' said Dave. 'Why can't I stay?'

'The living room, Davey,' Mum insisted. 'Now.'

Dave snorted in disgust, shoved back his chair and stamped into the living room. Why me? he thought. What did this happen to me for? If it was going to happen to anybody, it should have happened to Brain Damage. Or Costello. That would give everybody a break. It was so unfair. How come the bad things always seem to happen to the good guys?

'Yes,' he said aloud. 'Why me?'

He could hear raised voices coming from the kitchen. It was mostly Mum at first, then it was Dad's turn. It wasn't much of a discussion. More a shouting match. They seemed to be talking over each other's voices, neither one of them prepared to listen to what the other had to say.

'Oh, I'm going to work!' Dad barked finally.

Dave saw him stride down the hall to the front door. He stormed out without even saying goodbye to Mum. It was a long way from their usual kiss on the cheek.

'We'll talk properly when you've calmed down,' he shouted as a parting shot.

'When *I've* calmed down!' Mum retorted angrily. 'You'd think—'

She didn't get to finish. Dad slammed the door, started the car and drove off. The tyres squealed angrily as he pulled away. Dave watched the brake lights come on at the Give Way at the top of the street, then the car turning right towards Rice Lane.

'Are you ready, Davey?' Mum called.

'Yes.' It was all he could do to answer her.

'You've nothing extra to take?'

'No.'

Mum appeared in the doorway. 'Is that all you can say? Yes and no?'

Dave shrugged.

'So what's got into you?' Mum demanded. 'I hope you're not taking lessons off *him*.' She had her hands on her hips. She was still angry with Dad and it was carrying over into her conversation with Dave.

'Nothing,' said Dave. 'I'm fine.'

'Is it because your dad and me have had a few words?'

'A few?' said Dave with a mocking laugh.

'OK, so we had a bit of a row. We're … concerned.'

Dave noticed that she was choosing her words carefully. For his benefit, probably.

'No need,' said Dave. 'I feel fine.'

'I think I'll walk down the road with you,' said Mum. 'Just in case.'

'No way!'

'It's for your own good.'

'I'll feel a right divvy.'

'It's better than ending up—'

'Ending up what?' cried Dave. 'Dead?'

Mum shook her head. 'Now you're being dramatic.'

'Me?' Dave was speechless. *She* decides to re-enact

the Battle of Hastings with Dad, and then accuses *me* of being dramatic! 'Oh, please Mum. Don't come to school with me. Everybody'll skit me.'

He was just thankful that Brain Damage and Costello didn't go to Our Lady's. They attended Cropper Lane. At least he was spared a confrontation with the Demon Duo.

'I'll be straight up to that school if they do,' said Mum.

Dave looked imploringly at her. 'Please let me go on my own. Nobody in Year Six comes with their mum. I'd feel dead stupid.'

'I know that son, but—'

'I'll take care,' said Dave, sensing weakness. 'Besides, Jimmy's going to walk down with me.'

'Ronnie Mintoe's nephew?'

'That's right. He phoned last night when you were at the supermarket.'

He was on to a winner. Besides managing the Diamonds, Ronnie was a fireman and he'd been a local councillor for a while. Mum had a lot of time for the Mintoes. In her eyes they were the salt of the Earth.

'OK, OK,' she conceded. 'But I've written you a note.'

Dave smelt a rat. 'To say why I was off, you mean?'

'And to excuse you from PE.'

A rat! More a plague of the things. He loved PE. 'Miss PE! Why?'

'Do I really have to spell it out?'

'Yes.'

'You've just had a black-out. I don't want you doing anything that might be dangerous.'

'Oh Mum ...'

'Oh Mum nothing. I've given in to you over walking

to school. In return, you've got to sit out PE. Just until you get these tests done.'

Dave weighed the options. 'I suppose so.'

'Good,' said Mum. 'That sounds like Jimmy at the door now. Take care. And don't forget, the moment you feel a bit funny you sit down and ask for help.'

'Yeah yeah.'

Mum gave him a long stare, then handed him his bag. 'Bye, son.'

Dave nodded morosely. 'Sure, whatever.'

'And have a nice day.'

As he reached the front door he muttered under his breath. 'Nice day? Fat chance of that.'

But for Brain Damage and Costello it was a very nice day indeed. At last they seemed to have made a breakthrough in their campaign against the Diamonds. As Jimmy accompanied a quiet and serious Dave Lafferty to school, the enemy were engaged in horse-play at the top of Owen Avenue, waiting for their mates.

'Have you got the stuff?' asked Costello.

Brain Damage patted his school bag. 'Yes, nicked my dad's out of the bathroom cabinet. This is cool. Lafferty's really going to hate it.'

'I hope so. I want to see him squirm. Same as he did when you battered him.'

Brain Damage grinned broadly. He liked being reminded about his knock-out victory over Lafferty.

'And you're sure Our Lady's finishes at half past three?' Costello asked, not for the first time that morning.

'Sure I'm sure.'

'Brilliant,' said Costello. 'That gives us a quarter of an hour to get over there after ours lets out. Just make sure you don't get into any trouble today. We don't want to be kept back or anything.'

'For this,' said Brain Damage, 'I'll be a complete angel.'

Costello wrinkled his nose. 'No sense going over the top,' he said, 'quiet will do.'

'Quiet you've got,' said Brain Damage. He unzipped his bag and looked inside. 'This is going to be boss,' he chuckled. 'It really is.'

Three

That afternoon after school, Kev, Bash and Jamie were waiting at the school gates. The idea was to challenge Brain Damage and Costello over the attack on Dave. There was just one problem – the gang had already gone. They'd been the first out of school, and at that very moment they were gathering outside Our Lady's, five minutes walk away. Inside, unaware of their presence, Dave was also in a good mood. He was lining up in the corridor with Jimmy. They'd been sitting their maths tests and he thought he'd done quite well.

'Did you do the one about the supermarket trolley?' Dave asked.

'Joking, aren't you?' said Jimmy. 'That was rock hard.'

'It was only multiplication, you know,' said Dave. 'And we were allowed to use our calculators. You should have had a go.'

'Didn't look like timeses to me,' said Jimmy doubtfully.

'That's because you didn't read the question properly.'

Jimmy grimaced. Nobody likes a know-all. Dave registered the look on his mate's face. Time to change the subject.

'St Pat's this Sunday, isn't it?'

'That's right, they're just above us in the league. We could have done with you in the side, though. We're pretty short on firepower without you.'

'Well, you're going to have to sort something out,' said Dave. 'It's next week before I get this stupid brain test done. Mum wants me wrapped up in cotton wool till then. As if a game of footy or a bit of PE will do any harm.'

'You wouldn't have been playing anyway,' said Jimmy. 'You're not allowed, are you? On account of this School of Excellence.'

Dave winced visibly. 'Not much chance of that now.'

'Why not?'

'My black-out, divvy, that's why not.'

'My sister faints sometimes,' Jimmy objected, 'and it doesn't stop her doing things.'

'Maybe.'

Dave didn't want to be encouraged. He was feeling sorry for himself and nothing was going to shake him out of it. Not yet, anyway.

'It doesn't,' Jimmy insisted. 'Our Lisa does as she likes.'

'So what are they like, these faints of hers?'

'She just goes a bit woozy and has to sit down.'

'That all?'

Jimmy nodded.

'Then I think I did a bit more than faint,' said Dave.

Jimmy shrugged his shoulders. There was no pleasing some people.

Brain Damage and Luke Costello were continuing their

impatient vigil at the gates of Our Lady's. They had Tez Cronin in tow.

'They should be out by now,' said Costello, checking his watch. 'Are you sure you got the time right, Andy?'

'Positive.'

'Give us the can, then.'

'What, already?'

'Why not? They'll be here in a second.'

Brain Damage unzipped his bag and tossed the aerosol can over. Costello winked and pressed the nozzle. Tez and Brain Damage watched as he put plan 'Get Lafferty' into operation, then roared with appreciative laughter.

Dave was at the gates before he noticed them.

'Hey, Lafferty,' came a voice. 'What have you got, rabies?'

Dave turned towards the shout.

'Maybe it's mad cow disease,' came another voice. Brain Damage's. 'That it, Lafferty, been eating too many beefburgers?'

'Oh, you're sick,' said Jimmy, seeing what Costello and Co were up to.

Dave didn't say anything. Facing him were Costello, Brain Damage and Tez. Each of them had squirted shaving foam into their mouths and they were slobbering it all over their chins.

'I reckon he's just a nutter,' said Costello, spraying gobs of the stuff. 'Only nutters froth at the mouth. Hear me, Lafferty? You're a nutter. *Nutter!*'

Dave tried to shove past. 'Get lost.'

It was Brain Damage's turn. 'Nutters do foam at the mouth, don't they, Luke?'

Dave found his way barred.

'That's right. Andy. White stuff everywhere, like

mad dogs. That's because they're nutters. *Nutter!*

'Come on, Dave,' said Jimmy, taking him by the arm. 'Take no notice.'

'How do you do the shakes again, Lafferty?' asked Brain Damage. 'Like this, isn't it?' He mimicked the convulsions he'd witnessed at South Road.

'No,' said Tez. 'It goes more like this.' His plump body went into even more exaggerated spasms.

'Funny,' said Costello. 'I thought it was more like this.' He staggered into Dave, his whole body a-quiver. 'It's a nutter's dance, isn't that right … *Nutter!*'

Dave backed away. 'Leave me alone.'

But the stammered plea just made them worse. It was exactly what they'd been after, the slightest sign of weakness.

'Leave you alone?' sneered Costello. 'We'll never leave you alone, *Nutter.*'

'Dead right,' said Brain Damage. 'I did this to you. And you know what Lafferty, I can do it whenever I want. I have the power.'

And that was all Dave could take. With a cry of exasperation, he shoved Brain Damage aside and ran off down the road.

'Dave,' cried Jimmy. 'Hey, Dave, wait for me.'

'You won't catch him now,' said Costello, twisting the knife. 'The yellow get's running like a rabbit.'

'I'll give you yellow,' said Jimmy angrily, before setting off after Dave.

Costello watched him fleeing down the road. 'Well,' he said as he wiped the shaving foam from his face. 'We certainly rattled Lafferty's cage.'

'Not half,' said Brain Damage.

'And I liked that about you having the power. You know, I actually think he swallowed it.'

Brain Damage was beaming with satisfaction. 'He

did, didn't he?'

Which made the whole gang roar with laughter.

'To tell you the truth,' Costello gloated as the guffaws subsided. 'I don't think it could have gone much better.'

'Dave,' Jimmy shouted, as he crossed the railway bridge on to the Diamond. 'Where are you?' He shielded his eyes against the afternoon sun. No sign.

'You must have shifted,' Jimmy thought out loud. 'I didn't think I was this far behind. Trust you to do your Linford Christie on me.'

He slowed to a walk and resigned himself to Dave's disappearance. Maybe it was for the best. Let him calm down. Sort his head out. Jimmy decided to take the short-cut home, down the litter-strewn path that ran along the railway. As he jogged down the stone steps from the bridge he noticed something that made his heart flip. A boy was lying on the ground, his head bent at an awkward angle to the rest of his body. He was jerking and twitching.

Dave.

Four

This again, thought Dave. Answer questions. Watch the ceiling.

'I hate hospitals.'

'What's that, David?'

Dave closed his eyes for a second. The nurse wasn't supposed to hear that.

'He said,' the porter told her helpfully, 'he hates hospitals.'

'Oh,' said the nurse. 'Well, that makes two of us.'

'How come?'

'Because I'm here till nine tonight.'

Dave pulled a face. Ask a stupid question.

'So why do *you* hate hospitals?'

Dave shrugged his shoulders. 'Dunno. I just do, that's all.' Which is when he saw the sign above his head: *X-ray Department*. Dave was wheeled on his trolley to a high, narrow table in front of a machine that looked like a tunnel cut in half.

'Climb up on here,' said the nurse.

Dave did as he was told.

'Hello, David,' said a woman in a white coat. 'My name's Julie. I'm the radiologist.'

'You what?'

'I take pictures of the inside of your head.'

'Oh.'

I wish I hadn't asked, thought Dave.

'Now,' said Julie White-Coat, 'to do this we have to keep your head very still, so I'm going to fasten this strap across your forehead.'

'Like the electric chair,' said Dave.

'A bit,' said Julie.

'They say you can smell yourself cooking on the electric chair,' said Dave. He didn't know why he said it. It just came out.

'Well, you've no need to worry,' said Julie. 'I haven't cooked a kid since ... oh, Tuesday.'

'You did fry that girl from Linacre Lane,' joked the porter. 'Left here like a Bowyer's sausage, she did.'

'Oh yes,' said Julie. 'I forgot. Poor little banger.'

Dave felt the strap tighten round his head. For some reason the sensation brought the gang to mind. At the thought of their mocking laughter Dave found himself wincing.

'Not too tight, is it?' asked Julie.

'No.'

How could he explain about Brain Damage's power. Doctors don't believe in voodoo.

'Now, I've just got to pop these at the side of your face.' Julie attached two pads. 'Comfy?'

Dave almost nodded, but he thought better of it. 'Yes.'

'Now keep your head lovely and still,' said Julie.

For a couple of minutes she fiddled with a light above his head and the table he was lying on. Finally satisfied that she'd got him in the position she wanted, Julie leant over. 'I'm going into a room over there,' she explained. 'That's where the control panel is. I'll talk to you through an intercom.'

'OK.'

As the staff left, Dave felt suddenly alone. Like when he was about to take a penalty. He imagined himself standing there with the ball at his feet and wondered – if he really was taking a penalty, would he score?

'Right, David,' came Julie's voice. 'I'm going to start the machine. Keep really still.'

There was a whirring noise and Dave slid into the semi-circular tunnel. Moments later the machine started operating.

Click whirr, click whirr, click whirr.

It went on for two or three minutes.

Click whirr, click whirr, click whirr.

Then footsteps.

'That was great, David,' said Julie. 'Now, I'm just going to have to move you slightly.'

More fiddling.

'That's fine. Same procedure again. Keep nice and still.'

Dave looked up and saw the machine revolving.

Click whirr, click whirr, click whirr.

More fiddling. More clicking and whirring. Then it was all over.

'There,' said Julie, unfastening the strap. 'That wasn't too bad, was it?'

This time Dave could shake his head without getting into trouble. He thought about the penalty. Him with his foot on the ball and Brain Damage psyching him out from the touch-line. Would he score?

Five minutes later Dave was back on the ward. At least it hadn't hurt. He found himself smiling. Then it came back, the loneliness. He'd started to hate being on his own. It was the time he was forced to think about his black-outs. And Brain Damage. And the power. He found himself thinking about taking the penalty. Three steps back. Look at the ball. Then Brain Damage's voice: 'I can do it any time I like. I have the power.'

That's when Dave knew. The way things were going he knew exactly what he'd do.

Miss.

Five

It was the following Wednesday before Dave Lafferty returned to school.

'Look,' said Melanie Mulcahy half-way through Music. 'It's Dave.'

Jimmy couldn't believe his eyes. Dave had arrived, but that wasn't all. With him was his mum. They were crossing the yard, huddled behind an umbrella in the driving rain. Definitely odd, thought Jimmy, something had to be up if Dave allowed his mum to walk him to school.

'Take out your class readers for a couple of minutes,' said Mr Chappell, placing his beater on the xylophone. 'I need to have a quick word with Mrs Lafferty.'

Jimmy was aware of Mr Chappell and Mrs Lafferty talking just outside the room, but it was impossible to make out what they were saying. Some of his classmates glanced round at him, expecting an explanation, but he just shrugged his shoulders and hid behind his book.

'Is Dave staying?' asked Melanie. 'I mean, does he have to go back in hospital or anything?'

Jimmy just carried on staring at the book.

'You don't fool me,' said Melanie. 'I know you're listening.'

The fact that the book was upside down was a bit of a giveaway.

'I don't know nothing, all right?' snapped Jimmy.

'Does that mean you do know something?' asked Melanie, nudging her friend Jacqui Bell. Jacqui giggled.

Jimmy snorted. Always the smart-Alec, that one. 'Don't be so nosy, Jaws,' said Jimmy.

Melanie had had the nickname for six weeks, ever since she had her teeth braced.

Jacqui looked as if she was going to add her two pennyworth, but Jimmy got in first. 'Same goes for you, Ding-Dong,' he told her.

Jacqui grimaced. She hated her nickname almost as much as Melanie hated hers.

The door creaked open, and the whole class looked up. Mr Chappell was walking to his desk and Dave was following him. Dave reminded Jimmy of the Sheriff in a Western when he walks into a saloon full of bad hombres. The hombres in Y6C were actually pretty good, but Dave was still looking uncomfortable. Jimmy heard footsteps outside the window. Mrs Lafferty was already struggling back across the yard, wrestling with her umbrella in the wind.

'I'm sure everybody's pleased to see that David's back with us,' said Mr Chappell.

Like everyone else, Jimmy was expecting a little speech or something. Instead, Mr Chappell simply pointed to Dave's chair. 'Sit yourself down, lad. We'll get on with the lesson.'

And that was it.

'You OK?' Jimmy whispered.

'I'm fine.'

'But what did the hospital say?'

Mr Chappell was looking in their direction.

'I'll tell you after,' said Dave.

'Epilepsy, what's that?'

Dave could have just about coped with Jimmy, but he didn't want the rest of the class crowding round him the moment they got out on the yard. He suddenly knew how monkeys in a zoo felt.

'The electric signals in my brain are going funny,' said Dave. He had this planned. He would tell it more or less the way Dr Choudhury had told it to him.

'You what?' Melanie laughed out loud, but only for a few seconds. She was still self-conscious about her brace so she didn't like having her mouth open for long.

'It's like your teeth, I suppose.'

Melanie curled her top lip over the offending wires.

'They're a bit crooked, aren't they?'

Melanie blushed.

'Well,' Dave continued. 'They are, aren't they?'

Melanie nodded. She obviously wished she hadn't started this.

'So it's the same with my brain waves, according to the quacks.'

Jimmy frowned. 'I don't ...'

Dave sighed. He'd been preparing for this moment for days, but it didn't make it any less of a chore. 'The brain works by electricity, right?'

'Ye-es.'

'Well ...' How had Dr Choudhury put it? 'My electric signals get jumbled up. It makes me black out. They call it a seizure.'

'Does it hurt?' asked Melanie.

'Only when I laugh.'

'Can it kill you?' asked Jacqui.

Dave rolled his eyes. 'No, but *I* can kill *you* if you ask any more stupid questions.'

The other kids took the hint and melted away.

'That was a bit hard,' said Jimmy. 'They were only asking.'

'Well, I'm sick of people asking,' said Dave. 'It's bad enough being like this, without everybody going on about it.'

'Will you get better?'

'I don't think it works like that,' said Dave. 'I have to take tablets. One in the morning, one at night.'

'And that'll cure it?'

Suddenly all Dave could see was Brain Damage's leering face. 'Control it, maybe.' He closed his eyes to drive the grinning face from his mind. 'They can stop me having the seizures. I think ...'

Jimmy mulled it over in his mind. 'So you can still play footy?'

Dave lowered his eyes. No matter how hard he tried, he found Brain Damage's face and voice forcing themselves into his mind. Was it possible? Did he really have the power?

'You can, can't you?'

Dave shrugged his shoulders. 'I don't know if I want to.'

'What!' Jimmy was dumbfounded. Dave Lafferty not wanting to play footy!

Dave sucked in a deep breath. 'What did I look like, you know, when I had that fit?'

'It was over by the time I found you,' said Jimmy. He felt uncomfortable. He didn't know what to say.

'The first time, then,' said Dave. 'After the fight with Brain Damage.'

'It was a bit scary.'

'Go on,' said Dave. 'Why?'

'You were shaking. It's ... Well, it's not normal, is it?'

'No,' said Dave. 'It isn't.' He kicked at an empty drinks carton with the toe of his shoe. 'What about the dribbling?'

Jimmy stared at him questioningly.

'I was frothing at the mouth, wasn't I?'

'A bit, maybe.'

There was a silence, the sort you could drown in.

'Brain Damage says I looked like a mad dog.'

'Take no notice of that dweeb,' said Jimmy, tapping away at the drinks carton. 'He's the only mad dog round here. How come you arrived with your mum, anyway?'

'She had to force me to come to school,' Dave admitted after a pause. 'That's why I was late.'

'How come?'

'Do you think you'd come to school?' Dave demanded, 'if there was a chance everybody could see you ...' he was remembering Costello's crew with their shaving foam trick '... like that?'

'Dunno,' said Jimmy.

'Jimmy,' said Dave, still toying with the carton, 'do you believe in voodoo?'

'Come again?'

Dave felt suddenly foolish. 'Forget it. It's just that this epilepsy thing is getting to me.'

'Why? It's not your fault.'

Dave kicked the carton away. It was almost as if he was kicking away his life.

'Isn't it?'

Six

There was none of the usual banter in the Diamonds' dressing-room. They were too busy planning for the gang's arrival.

'Reckon they'll show?' asked Gord nervously. As a fighter, Gordon Jones would make a good flower arranger. He was a big lad but he was about as hard as rice pudding.

Kev hissed his answer. 'You don't think they'd miss this, do you? A chance to gloat about Dave. They'll be here, all right.'

'Have you heard how Dave is, Jimmy?' Daz asked, pulling on his padded goalkeeper's gloves.

'He's having tests,' came the reply. Jimmy sounded breathless. He'd been the last to arrive. 'Uncle Ronnie called on Dave's mum and dad last night.'

'What sort of tests?' asked Ratso, without looking up. He was fast forwarding the tape in his ghetto blaster, trying to find the Diamonds' latest anthem.

'Some sort of brain scan, I think,' said Jimmy. 'Ask Uncle Ronnie. He knows more about it than I do.'

'Why's that?' asked Daz.

'Our Mike,' said Jimmy, 'he was in hospital for ages after his accident. Ronnie was never out of the place.'

'What happened, anyway?'

'Haven't I told you?' asked Jimmy. 'Most of the lads already know. Mike was a bit of a tearaway. He was about eleven when it happened. Him and his mates were climbing on a factory roof, only Mike stood on a rotten bit and fell right through. Broke his back.'

Daz winced.

'Got it,' announced Ratso, who had been crouching on the dressing-room floor with his ear pressed to the speaker, oblivious to the conversation. 'Now we can take the field.'

'So what's the tune this week?' asked Jamie.

'"Ain't no stopping us now",' Ratso said, pressing the play button. 'Bit of a golden oldie. My mum picked it.'

The Diamonds listened.

'Like it?' asked Ratso.

'It'll do,' said Kev, grudgingly. 'Come on, lads, let's make our entrance.'

As they jogged on to the field, the Diamonds looked around for any sign of the gang, but they hadn't arrived yet.

'A bit blowy, eh, lads?' said the referee.

'Take your wig off,' quipped Kev, acknowledging him.

'It could help me with my long throws,' said Ant hopefully.

'Not yet,' said Kev. 'You heard what Ronnie said. It's a secret weapon. That means we only use it in emergencies.'

Gord couldn't care less about the wind, or Ant's throw-ins. He was more concerned about Costello's gang. 'Maybe they won't come,' he said hopefully.

'If you mean King Rat and his cronies,' Kev said, 'they'll be here, all right. And they're going to wish they hadn't bothered.'

'How do you mean?' asked Jimmy, frowning.

'We're going to sort them out,' said Ant. 'For what they did to Dave.'

Mattie Hughes grinned. 'There won't be enough pieces left to pick up.'

'Uncle Ronnie won't like it,' said Jimmy.

'Ronnie doesn't have to know,' said Guv. 'Unless somebody tells him.' He gave Jimmy a meaningful stare.

'This is stupid,' said Jimmy. 'Uncle Ronnie will blow his top.'

'Only if you go spilling your guts,' Kev replied. 'So just keep shtum. What you don't know can't hurt you.'

Jimmy wrinkled his nose. There was no way they were going to keep a major punch-up from his Uncle Ronnie.

'Shtum, remember,' Kev repeated, stabbing a finger in his direction to emphasize the point.

The Diamonds started lining up opposite St Pat's. Only Jimmy remained out of position. He glanced at Ronnie, then at Guv.

'Jimmy,' shouted Ronnie. 'Don't just stand there like a flipping lemon. Get over on the left where you belong.'

Jimmy nodded absent-mindedly and took up his position. The unease that had been grinding away inside him was mounting.

'Don't even think of mentioning it to Ronnie,' warned Ant, reading Jimmy's expression. 'Guv's right. Costello and Brain Damage deserve a good kicking for what they've done.'

'I don't know ...' Jimmy began dubiously.

'Well I do,' said Ant. 'There's no going back on it now. We're going to do them. So let's get on with the game. Call it a warm-up to the main action.'

As Ant moved away, Gord sidled up to Jimmy. 'I'm with you,' he whispered. 'Bash agrees as well. He just said so. This is bad news.'

'Yes,' Jimmy answered. 'I know. The only problem is: what do we do about it?'

There was no time to decide. The referee had blown and Guv and the St Pat's skipper were standing next to him.

'Call,' said the ref, tossing a ten pence piece.

'Heads,' said Kev.

'Heads it is.'

'Our kick-off then,' said Kev.

The St Pat's captain licked his finger and tested the air theatrically. 'We'll change round,' he said. 'We'll start with the wind at our backs.'

As Kev trotted away, he could feel his shirt pressing against his skin. The strong wind was definitely going to play a part. 'Come on, lads,' he shouted. 'Let's have some commitment. Two more games before the Cup final.'

His words seemed to do the trick, as all the early pressure came from the Diamonds. Bashir was getting a lot of freedom out on the left flank, and Kev and John were running things in the middle of the park.

As it turned out, the only thing missing was the killer touch up front. In Dave's absence, Jamie was playing as a lone striker and the threat was easily snuffed out by St Pat's well-organized trio of central defenders.

'This is no use,' Jamie panted, as yet another Diamonds' attack came to nothing. 'They're crowding me out.'

Kev looked thoughtful.

'So what do we do about it?' asked Jamie.

'Nothing,' said Kev. 'The breaks will come.'

They did, but for the wrong team. Having survived the expected Diamonds' onslaught and found it about as effective as feather dusters at 400 yards, St Pat's started to play themselves into the game. Half-way through the first half they got a corner.

'Stay on the back post,' Daz told John.

He may as well have saved his breath. Nerves were definitely jangling in the Diamonds' defence and it was leading to errors. As the corner came over Daz, Ant and John all rose to meet it.

'My ball!' Daz roared commandingly, but in their enthusiasm to clear it, his own defenders were baulking him.

With a loud *ouf* the Diamonds' keeper crashed to the ground. The unmarked St Pat's striker was able to take his time and slot the ball home. The Diamonds were one-nil down.

'You plank!' thundered Daz as he pursued a red-faced John O'Hara across the box. 'I thought I told you to stay on the back post.'

'I never heard you,' John answered feebly.

'Then hear this, Mr Gormless,' bawled Daz, right down his ear. 'Next time they get a corner, you do as you're told. Moron!'

'Cool it a bit, Daz,' said Kev. 'I know you like to dominate your box, but that was a bit over the top.'

'Good coming from you,' said Daz. He didn't appreciate the interference. Kev might be the Guv'nor but the goalmouth was his. Daz's law.

John slunk away to lick his wounds, but there was no time for sulking. Determined to build on their lead, St Pat's came right back at the Diamonds.

'Are you playing or what?' yelled Kev.

'What?' asked John.

'I'll give you what. Stay focused. We *are* losing, you know.'

John grimaced. Now who was being over the top? 'Sorry, Guv.'

'Defend, you divvies,' yelled Daz behind them. He always shouted at his defenders, but he really did look as if he was going to burst a blood vessel. 'Close them down! Close the beggars do-o-o-wn.'

Driven by Daz-power, Gord got in a sliding tackle and Bashir tidied up.

'That's more like it,' said Daz approvingly. 'Good to see somebody's paying attention to the play.'

It turned out to be a hairy few minutes for the Diamonds. They didn't have a presence up front to take the pressure off the midfield and defence. They were only able to keep the score down thanks to some desperate last-gasp defending and a crop of spectacular saves by Daz.

'Longmoor will love this,' said Kev, glancing across to Pitch Five where their Cup final opponents were playing. 'We're hanging on for dear life.'

St Pat's got their fourth corner.

'Now,' Daz said pointedly to John. 'Guard that back post. With your life. Stick to it like superglue, you hear?'

It was a well-taken corner. Daz came for it but in the crowded goalmouth he could only punch it as far as the penalty spot. He was still trying to get back to his line when one of the St Pat's forwards struck the ball on the volley. John managed to get a foot to the goal-bound shot and sliced it out of play for a throw-in.

'More like it,' said Daz. 'Though the clearance could have been directed better. See, that's why I wanted you on the post.'

As Daz walked away, John pulled a face. The praise was about as faint as it could get.

While the Diamonds tried to sort themselves out in defence, they got a rare break in attack. Playing as a wing-back, Joey intercepted the throw-in and scampered away down the right wing.

'Give us it!' shouted Kev. 'Square ball, square ball.'

Joey nodded and rolled it into the path of the Diamonds' captain. Kev took it in his stride and ran on, leaving his marker for dead. Bashir was making a promising forward run to his left.

'Bash.'

Kev side-footed the ball into the space behind the full-back and watched with satisfaction as Bashir outpaced his man and took the ball to the line.

'Get it over,' cried Kev. 'First time.'

Bashir looked up and hit the ball low and hard across the goalmouth. Jamie attempted a diving header but mis-timed his leap. He ended up clumsily chesting it in.

One-all.

'Bit of a fluke,' said Jamie, picking himself up. It hadn't lived up to his vision of a cannonball header.

'Don't worry about it,' said Kev. 'They all count.'

Play had hardly re-started when the whistle went for half-time.

'It doesn't look like they're going to turn up, after all,' said Gord as the Diamonds left the field.

'Gord,' Kev told him. 'Forget it, will you? If you're scared then leave it to the rest of us.'

'Scared?' Gord repeated. 'Who said I was scared?' He followed Ratso to the touch-line. 'You don't think I'm scared, do you?' Gord asked.

'Nah,' said Ratso.

Gord smiled. Good old Ratso.

'Terrified's more like it.'

At the start of the second half the Diamonds took the field to loud jeering.

'Here they are,' said Kev, quietly noting the gang's arrival. 'Better late than never.' There was a touch of satisfaction in his voice. He had his mind on events *after* the match.

'Oh,' sighed Gord, nervously clocking Costello and Brain Damage. 'Er ... good. We'll give them what for, won't we, Guv?' But he couldn't disguise the shake in his voice.

Kev and Ant gave him a look of utter contempt and jogged lightly on the spot, waiting for the re-start.

'Like to take the first pop at them, would you, Gord?'

Gord didn't answer Kev. He might just mean it.

St Pat's launched the second half, but their passing immediately let them down. Intercepting an attempted cross, Ant booted the ball back upfield. Assisted by the strengthening wind, the ball carried almost into St Pat's penalty area. It was a chase between Bashir and the keeper. As it turned out, it was no contest. The little winger scampered in, flicking the ball deftly over the goalie's despairing lunge.

Two-one to the Diamonds.

'We'll coast it now,' said Mattie.

For a few minutes that's how the Diamonds played. Like they had the game sewn up and it was just a matter of playing out time. It was a high-risk strategy and Kev knew it.

'Don't just sit back,' he yelled, berating John for a casual back-pass that almost let St Pat's in. 'If we take our foot off the pedal we could let them back into this.'

His words were prophetic. A couple of minutes later Ant was strolling forward with the ball at his feet. He decided to stroke the ball out to Jimmy, but his pass was feeble.

'You wally!' shrieked Kev as the nearest St Pat's forward sprang on the ball.

Ant tried to recover but the attacker skipped over his flailing tackle and ran on. Left completely exposed by his defence, Daz had no choice but to come out. As he tried to rush the oncoming attacker, Daz prayed that the lad wouldn't have the presence of mind to chip him. He prayed in vain, having to watch in agony as the ball sailed over his head and dropped into the net.

Two-all.

'What did I say?' snapped Kev as the jubilant laughter of Costello and Co rang tauntingly in his ears.

'Sorry, Guv,' said Ant. 'It was my fault.'

'I know whose rotten fault it was,' Kev told him.

But still the Diamonds didn't snap out of their torpor. Five minutes later it was Joey who gave the ball away. St Pat's seized on the unforced error. A perfect exchange of passes and the ball was in the net. Some goals seem to happen in slow motion. This one was scored on fast forward.

'I don't believe it,' groaned Kev. 'We're three-two down.'

The gang believed it. They were shouting sarcastic remarks from the touch-line.

'Nice one, Joey. You ought to be wearing a St Pat's jersey.'

'That's one thing you can say about the Diamonds – generous to a fault.'

'Heard the one about the Diamonds player who passed to his own side. No, neither have I!'

And more of the same ilk.

'I'm going to bury them,' snarled Kev.

'Not if I get to them first,' said Ant grimly.

Jimmy listened gloomily and looked over at Uncle Ronnie. He was kneeling down, chatting to Michael and laughing. Jimmy wasn't. It was decision time.

'What's Jimmy up to?' asked Ant, noticing the full-back hovering close to the touch-line.

Kev's eyes narrowed. As Jimmy returned from his hasty conversation with Ronnie, Kev challenged him. 'What was that about?'

But Jimmy was ready for him. He'd been planning his answer. 'Uncle Ronnie called me over. He reckons you're playing too deep.'

'So why didn't he tell me himself?' demanded Kev. 'I am the club captain.'

'He couldn't get your attention,' said Jimmy. 'The wind, I suppose.'

Kev wasn't completely convinced, but he accepted the tactical change. Within a minute, it was paying dividends. Kev linked up with Jamie and almost put him through on goal.

'More like it,' shouted Ronnie encouragingly.

It was the Diamonds' turn to press. Kev was suddenly in complete charge, spraying passes out to Bashir and Jamie and drawing defenders with his forward runs. His presence had an unsettling effect on St Pat's.

'Guv,' shouted John, breaking forward.

Kev responded without a moment's hesitation, punting the ball forward. Again the wind played its part, carrying the ball over the St Pat's centre-backs. John was left with only the goalie to beat and rifled it in from ten yards.

Three-all.

With two minutes to go the Diamonds took the lead. Unable to stop Kev's raids fairly, his marker was tackling recklessly. It was only a matter of time before he got punished for it. The breakthrough came when Kev drove forward from his own centre circle and was brought down on the edge of the penalty area. It was left to Jamie to convert the resulting free-kick and he didn't let the Diamonds down.

Four-three.

'See the bend on that?' cried Ratso. 'A touch of the Carlos Roberto. We don't wear the yellow of Brazil for nothing.'

But if they were capable of Brazil-style attacking, the Diamonds were also prone to San Marino-style blunders in defence. This time Gord was the culprit. He'd noticed the ref raising his whistle to his mouth and relaxed for a moment, expecting him to blow.

'Gord,' yelled Kev. 'Who do you think you're marking?'

Alerted to the threat, Gord looked round. To his horror, the St Pat's forward had at least two yards on him. Unable to make up the distance, Gord could only watch as his man curled it inside the far post. At the final whistle the arrival of the Longmoor Celtic team made the Diamonds' misery complete.

'What was the score?' asked Nosmo.

'Four-all,' sighed Jamie.

'We won six-nil,' gloated Nosmo. 'See you soon.'

Nosmo's best mate, a lad the Diamonds only knew as Skinhead, couldn't resist a parting dig. 'When do we batter them first?' he asked. 'In the league or the cup?'

'League,' said Nosmo. 'Once we've got a solid victory under our belt in that, we'll really open up in the Cup final. Pay-back times two.'

The Diamonds watched Longmoor striding away. They looked confident.

'Still,' said Jamie. 'At least we didn't lose.'

'It feels like we did,' said Kev, scowling at the catcalls coming from Costello's gang. 'Fancy throwing it away like that. I bet Longmoor think the Cup's theirs already.'

'Forget it,' said Ant, slapping Kev on the shoulder. 'We've bigger fish to fry.'

Kev looked in the direction of the gang. 'Come on,' he said. 'Let's get them.'

Seven

'Just our luck,' grumbled Ant. 'They're getting straight off.'

'Isn't that a shame?' said Gord, unconvincing as ever. 'I was just getting warmed up ready.' But relief that he wouldn't have to fight was flooding through him.

'Come on, lads,' said Kev, ignoring him. 'What are you waiting for? Let's get them.'

Gord went white. Just when he thought he was off the hook.

'What about our kit?' asked Ant. 'We'll have to go back for it first.'

'I've already got that sorted,' said Kev. 'Carl's going to watch it for us while we sort those lousy toe-rags.'

'Does he need help?' asked Gord. 'Carl, I mean?'

Ant winked at Kev. 'What do you reckon, Guv?'

'Go on, Gordy,' said Kev. 'You can join him on guard duty.'

'Cheers, Guv,' said a delighted Gord.

As he raced off Ant poked Kev in the back. 'You know what?' he said. 'You're just a big softy.'

'You'll soon see who's a softy,' Kev answered quietly.

Costello and Brain Damage were walking through Jacob's Lane car park when they heard their names being called.

'In a hurry or something?'

They turned to face Kev. 'No, why?'

'Because we want a word with you.'

Brain Damage crossed his arms. 'We're listening.'

'That was a lousy trick you pulled against Dave Lafferty,' said Kev. 'He's back in hospital, and it's all down to you.'

'Aw,' said Brain Damage. 'You're breaking my heart.'

Costello led the chorus of mocking laughter.

'Shut it,' said Kev. 'Or I'll come over and shut it for you.'

'You and whose army?' asked Costello.

'Me,' Kev replied, indicating the rest of the team, 'and this army.'

With Carl and Gord watching their gear and Jimmy and Bashir refusing to have anything to do with the fight, there were eight of the Diamonds present, as opposed to six in Costello's gang. Kev wasn't counting his chickens yet, though. Daz wasn't the sort to get into a punch-up unless he was provoked. And the provocation had to be pretty bad. Unscrewing his knee-cap without permission, that sort of thing. Everybody called him the gentle giant. What's more, Joey usually went along with Daz. So most likely it was going to be six against six.

'Just do one,' said Brain Damage derisively. He gestured with his hand, as if swatting a troublesome fly.

'I'll do you,' said Kev, stung by Brain Damage's off-hand reply. He advanced to within a few inches of his enemy.

'Come on, then.'

Kev accepted the offer. He seized Brain Damage by his jacket collar and forced him back over the bonnet of a car. But Brain Damage was ready. He brought his knee up and caught Kev squarely in the stomach. As the pain shot through him, Kev doubled up and relaxed his grip for a second. It gave Brain Damage the chance to roll off the bonnet and lash out with his balled fist.

'You'll have to do better than that,' said Kev, feinting back.

'What, like this?'

Brain Damage kicked at Kev's knee, but Kev was ready for him. His dad hadn't taught him much – he'd never been around long enough – but he was enough of a boxer's son to have picked up a few tricks.

'What are we waiting for?' yelled Ant. 'Don't leave Guv to do it all. Get them. This is for Dave Lafferty.'

But the fight was halted before it even got going.

'You're not getting anybody, Anthony.'

Kev turned to see Ronnie walking towards them. Mike was at his side pushing his wheelchair with those huge arms of his. George Rogan, and John and Daz's dads were only just behind. Jimmy was hovering in the background with Bashir.

'But they put Dave in hospital,' Kev protested.

'Two wrongs don't make a right,' said Ronnie. 'Besides, it wasn't the fight that brought on Dave's attack. Not according to Mrs Lafferty.'

'You don't expect us to believe that, do you?' asked Kev.

'You can believe what you like,' said Ronnie. 'I'm just telling you what the doctors think.'

'Well, I know exactly who's to blame,' said Ant, fixing Brain Damage with an icy stare. 'Somebody's got to sort them out.'

'And that somebody is you, I suppose,' said Ronnie.

'Yes, why not?'

'Because it'll get you into a lot of hot water,' said Mike.

'And,' George Rogan added, 'because any lad who takes this further will be suspended from the league ... indefinitely.'

'Oh, come off it,' said Kev, 'this isn't our fault.'

'I didn't say it was,' George replied. 'I'm just telling you as clearly as I can that the league won't allow fighting.'

Brain Damage and Costello were smirking. Things couldn't have gone any better if they'd planned it.

'You mean you're going to let them get away with it?' asked Kev, completely outraged.

'I mean,' George replied calmly, 'any boy caught fighting in these grounds will be breaking the league's rules and will no longer be considered a registered player.'

Kev saw the enemy grinning from ear to ear. He wanted to go over and wipe the smiles off their faces. 'But that isn't fair! They started it.'

'No we never,' said Costello. 'You followed us, remember.'

'Only because of what he did to Dave.' Kev was pointing at Brain Damage.

'Put another record on, McGovern,' said Brain Damage. 'You're getting boring.'

'I think you'd better leave,' said Ronnie. 'Pronto.'

Costello and Brain Damage led the way, but as if to show their contempt for the Diamonds, they sauntered with calculated slowness. Kev watched them depart, his throat tight with frustration.

Satisfied that everything was settled, George walked back on to the playing-fields. 'I'll leave you to talk to your boys, Ron,' he said.

'Don't worry, George,' said Ronnie. 'There'll be no repetition.'

'Thanks a bunch, Ronnie,' Kev snarled, the moment George was out of sight. 'And you, Jimmy. I had a feeling you were going to rat on us.'

Jimmy turned away.

'You listen to me, Kevin,' Ronnie said, 'one more incident like this and I'll report you to George personally. That doesn't just go for Jacob's Lane either. If I hear that you've carried this on with those lads, then you're out of my team. Got that?'

There was a long silence.

'I asked you a question, Kevin. Have you got that?'

Kev stared at the ground. He was aware of the other boys waiting for his answer.

'Yes.'

Eight

A week later, the Diamonds were battling for their lives against a Longmoor side that had taken the field thirsting for revenge.

'Get a grip,' Kev told his defence. 'They're ripping us to shreds.'

The game was only half-way through the second half and the Diamonds were already three-one down. Costello and Brain Damage were leading their gang in jeering every mistake the Diamonds made. Ronnie had already made a couple of appeals to them to cut it out, but with little effect.

'You don't need to tell *us* that,' Ant growled as Daz picked the ball out of the net. 'We're the ones on the receiving end back here. What about my long throw-in? You can't say *this* isn't an emergency.'

'Oh, shut up about your long throw-in,' said Kev.

Ant scowled. He was feeling pretty sore with Kev and the way he dismissed the idea of letting him try his long throw just added to his irritation. It was the way he'd sent Jimmy to Coventry over grassing them up to Ronnie. Everybody else had made their peace with Jimmy. Not Kev. He just wouldn't forget it. It had soured things in the dressing-room and it wasn't doing much for teamwork on the field.

'Well, tighten it up at the back,' said Kev.

'Yessir!' said Ant, standing stiffly to attention and saluting sarcastically.

'You trying to be funny?' asked Kev.

'There's nothing funny about getting battered,' Ant shot back.

Kev walked away shaking his head. 'You're cracking up, Ant,' he murmured.

'Yes, and *he*'s cracking me up,' Ant told Gord.

Immediately after the re-start the Diamonds lost possession again, gifting it to Nosmo in the centre circle. Nosmo took route one and headed for goal. Blocked by Ant and Gord, the big midfielder turned and rolled the ball back to Skinhead. To everybody's surprise Skinhead shot from all of thirty yards. The ambitious effort looked to be going wide when it took a wicked deflection off Jimmy's back. The sudden change of direction wrong-footed the whole defence. In slow motion the ball bounced into the net past a stranded Daz Kemble.

'Brilliant,' said Kev sarcastically as Jimmy sank to the ground. 'Trust you to get in the way. Sure you didn't do it on purpose?'

'You what?' said Jimmy, stung by the injustice of the remark. 'Take that back.'

But Kev wasn't in the mood to make any sort of sense, never mind apologize. The red mist was clouding his judgement. Burning with humiliation he raged on. 'I said: only a complete div like you would go for a shot like that. It was way off target.'

Jimmy had turned white with anger. 'The ball hit me,' he said. 'Got that? *It* hit *me*. I was trying to get out of the way.'

'Well, try a bit harder next time,' said Kev. 'We're four-one down.'

'Oh, get stuffed.'

Kev's eyes narrowed. 'Say that again,' he snarled. 'Go on, you just repeat it and I'll flatten you.'

Ratso looked towards the touch-line. The expression on his face said it all: Kev's lost it. Get him off.

'Kevin!' came Ronnie's voice.

Kev looked round.

'Yes, you Kevin,' shouted Ronnie. 'You're off.'

Kev's mouth dropped open. 'Me?'

'Yes, you.' Ronnie slapped Carl Bain on the shoulder. 'On you go, Carl. Ant, you take over as captain.'

As Kev trudged from the field, Costello's gang closed on him.

'Nothing down for you now, McGovern.'

'Better admit it, you've had it in the final.'

'I'm going to love watching Celtic roast you again.'

Kev turned away. 'What did you take me off for, Ronnie?' he demanded.

'This stupid thing with Jimmy, that's what for. If

there's one thing we don't need in the run-up to the final, it's a civil war in the team.'

'You wouldn't have taken me off if it had been anybody else I was arguing with.'

'Meaning?'

'He's your nephew. Says it all, doesn't it.'

'Now that's stupid talk, Kev,' said Mike. 'You know my dad better than that.'

But Ronnie was quite capable of fighting his own battles. His eyes blazed with anger. 'You can apologize for that, Kevin. Now.'

Kev stared. 'Never.'

'Well,' the normally placid Ronnie stormed, 'if that's your attitude you can go and get your kit.'

Kev looked shaken. 'You're joking!'

But Ronnie had lost it in a big way. 'Joking, am I? You've got your marching orders. Do I make myself clear?'

'But ...'

Ronnie didn't lose his temper often, but when he did he really blew.

'That's a bit harsh,' said Mike.

Ronnie wiped his brow. A hint of doubt was beginning to creep across his face. But Kev had gone. He didn't stop to argue or to watch the rest of his side's humiliation. He just carried on walking. Past Ronnie, past Michael in his wheelchair, past the gang and on into the changing-rooms. With Ronnie's angry words echoing in his head, he stared round at the tiled walls. As he peeled off his beloved yellow shirt he wondered if he would ever wear it again.

'What's going on?' came a familiar voice.

The Diamonds didn't even look up. Their heads were down and that's how they looked like staying.

'Dave,' said Jimmy. 'It's you!'

Jimmy wasn't the only one to greet Dave's arrival. The gang were already on their feet, pulling faces and mouthing the usual abuse.

'Yes,' said Dave, doing his best to ignore them. 'Dad persuaded me to come down. Said I couldn't mope round the house forever.'

'Tell you what,' said Jimmy, 'we could do with you out there today.'

'Why, what's the score?'

'We're four-one down and it's only half-time.'

Dave ran his eyes over the dispirited team. 'Where's Guv?'

'Cleared off,' said Jimmy. 'Just like you did that time.'

Dave pursed his lips. 'That was when Bobby Jones was manager. So what got into Guv?'

'Him and Jimmy had a bust-up,' said Ant by way of explanation. 'Guv got substituted.'

'Guv taken off?' said Dave. 'He wouldn't like that.'

'He didn't.'

'Is this still over you telling on him?'

Jimmy nodded ruefully.

'Got a long memory, hasn't he?'

'Not half,' said Jimmy. 'He's been looking right through me, then he started with the sarcy comments.'

'It's a bummer for the Diamonds, though,' said Dave. 'Hard to see us clawing three goals back without him.'

'We'd stand a chance with you playing,' said Ratso.

'That's right,' said Bashir. 'You haven't started with Everton yet, have you?'

Dave shook his head. 'It's not that.' For all his efforts to block out Brain Damage and the gang, the constant barrage was getting to him. 'I just can't.'

'Why not?' asked Ratso.

'Forgotten already, have you?' said Dave. 'You saw the state of me.'

'But you're on those tablets, aren't you?' asked Jimmy. 'Why not just give it a go?'

'Yes,' shouted Costello. 'Have a go. You can give us all a laugh.'

Dave coloured. 'Can't.'

'Go on.'

'I can't,' cried Dave. 'I don't know what I came down here for. I've had it with footy. I can't play again. I just can't.'

Jimmy saw the boys stirring ready for the second half. 'Come on, Dave,' he said, glaring at the gang as their catcalls built to a crescendo. 'Don't go over the top. They can't hurt you. You can do this. I know you can.'

Alerted by Dave's obvious discomfort, Ronnie had begun to show an interest in their conversation.

'Then you know more than me,' said Dave. 'Forget it.'

'But—'

'Leave the lad alone,' advised Ronnie. 'You can't make him play if he doesn't want to.'

Dave lowered his eyes. He knew he was letting his mates down, but there was no way he could have pulled on the Diamonds jersey that morning. Pictures kept flashing through his mind. Of him lying on the ground twitching, of the foam on his lips, of everyone shrinking back in horror. Most of all, of Brain Damage standing triumphantly over him. Playing was out of the question.

A loud roar made him snap out of his morbid thoughts for a moment. 'What was that?' he asked.

'Five-one,' said Mike. 'The lads are getting murder-ed.'

Dave knew his team-mates would be looking in his direction, but he turned away. He couldn't meet their eyes. No more than he could drive Brain Damage from his mind.

'I'm off, Ronnie,' he said. 'This was a mistake.'

From the half-way line Jimmy saw Dave taking the long walk towards Jacob's Lane. The second member of the team to walk away that morning.

Nine

It looks like I've done it this time. Jamie called round after the match. Eight-one the final score, and it could have been worse but for Daz in goal. According to Jamie he was a real hero, pulling off a string of saves. If it hadn't been for him we'd have been at the receiving end of a record defeat. Double figures humiliation. He even saved a penalty.

Jamie was almost spitting blood by the time he got to ours and he had a right go at me for storming off like that. He says I'm acting like a prima donna. There's more at stake than my pride, he says, there's the whole team to think about. I listened to what he had to say and I know he's right but sometimes right doesn't come into it. Some things you just don't do and going down on my hands and knees is one of them. Sorry's for wimps. I can't go grovelling to Ronnie, not even for the Diamonds. That just isn't my style. No, he'll have to make the first move. He was well out of order. OK, so I shot my mouth off a bit, but that's me. He knows that. But look what he did. Pulling me off was bad enough, but replacing me with a wombat like Carl Bain. That's a calculated insult!

This thing with Dave seems serious, too. I never thought he'd jack in football altogether. It's like Bugs Bunny losing interest in carrots. Maybe Davey's sicker than we all imagined. Funny things, brains. It's not like a sprained ankle. Suddenly, I feel like my whole world's crashing down. A month ago I thought we were heading for real success. Me and Dave were the two hearts of a great fighting unit. Look at the Diamonds now. The two hearts have stopped beating and it looks like there's nothing that can save the team. They're eleven condemned men and the executioner's sharpening his axe.

PART THREE

Injury Time

One

Ding ding ding.

Woof woof woof.

Oh, knock it off, Dixie, thought Dave as he waited impatiently on the doorstep, I'm not in the mood.

Ding ding ding.

Just quit barking, thought Dave, it's getting on my nerves.

Woof woof woof.

That's when Dave came to the conclusion that dogs are either very stubborn or just plain stupid.

'You're back early,' said Mum, opening the door and peering into the street. 'Nobody with you today?'

Once in a while Dave would bring some of his mates back after a match. Not this Sunday morning.

'So there's no cloud of human locusts to strip my fridge?' Mum asked light-heatedly. Or as light-heartedly as she could manage when Dave's 'problem' was never far from her mind. That was what she called it – the problem. She couldn't bring herself to say epilepsy. It was a constant source of friction between them.

'No.'

It was his leave-me-alone grunt. He felt like he didn't really have mates any more. No, worse than that. He had nothing. He was all alone with the problem – this thing in his head, this stifling darkness hiding somewhere inside waiting to rush over him again, to overwhelm and humiliate him.

'Are you OK?' Mum asked as Dave shoved past her and an almost hysterical Dixie.

Dave stopped. 'Of course I am. What made you say that?'

He could hear her taking a deep breath. Her way of controlling her temper.

'Oh, get down, Dixie,' he snapped as the little dog jumped up, his paws scrabbling about on his knees. 'Get off!'

'Davey!' cried Mum as he pushed Dixie roughly away.

'Well, I don't want him jumping up on me all the time,' said Dave, already a little ashamed at his show of temper.

'Something *is* wrong,' said Mum. 'I've seen you in a nark before, but I've never seen you take it out on poor Dixie.'

Drawn by the raised voices in the hallway, Dad appeared from the living room and quickly wished he hadn't.

'This was your idea,' Mum stormed at Dad. 'Give him some space, you said, let him go and see his mates. Well, look at the way he's come home. You're upset, aren't you, Davey?' she asked, turning her attention back to Dave. 'Is it those lads again?'

Dave's heart kicked. 'What makes you say that?'

She lowered her voice. 'You didn't—'

'No,' Dave interrupted, wondering why people always seemed to lower their voices when they mentioned it – the problem. It's not like he'd grown antennae or something. 'I haven't had a seizure. I'm fine.'

'You don't look it,' observed Mum. 'You're quite sure it isn't your problem?'

'Sure I'm sure,' said Dave, his irritation growing. 'One hundred per cent pigging wonderful, that's me. Look at me, I'm so rotten healthy I could puke.' And with that he ran upstairs to his room, leaving his parents to make sense of the outburst.

He wasn't even on the landing before the all-too-predictable row had erupted downstairs.

'And what was all that about?' Dad asked.

'You and your do-nothing attitude.'

'Come again?'

'Did you see the state of him? Give him his freedom, you said. Look where it got him.'

'You sent him to school, not me.'

'Oh, that's right. Throw that in my face.'

Dave hesitated outside his bedroom door. Freedom. That's what it was about, all right, but how could he ask for the freedom to do as he liked when there was nothing he *could* do? Run, cycle, walk – it would always be there waiting to bring him down.

'I think it's about time he got back into his old routine,' Dad was arguing. 'The Epilim's controlling the seizures. He might never have another.'

'And then again he might,' Mum retorted. 'Didn't you listen to what Dr Choudhury said? No cycling, no swimming. You can't wish this away. We've got to make allowances for his condition.'

'Dr Choudhury didn't say anything about football, did he?' Dad replied. 'Or rounders, or cricket, or going for a walk, or meeting his mates. And you're twisting the quack's words – Dave'll be OK swimming as long as there's somebody with him. Why have you got to act this way? I didn't hear Dr Choudhury say life was out of bounds.'

Trust Dad to go over the top, thought Davey from his vantage point on the landing.

'Oh, you're just being stupid,' said Mum. 'As usual.'

The *As usual* sounded fainter. She must have gone into another room. For a moment Dave strained to hear, but the row might as well have been in Serbo-Croat for all the sense it was making to him. Giving up on it, he walked into his room and flopped on his back on the bed. His swinging foot touched something on the floor.

'What's that?' he wondered out loud.

He rolled over on to his stomach and reached down to a cardboard box. The one that contained his footy programmes. Everton FC. He flicked through them then got up and opened his wardrobe. There, crisply ironed, were his first team replica kits. Blue and white home strip. Yellow and blue away strip. Then there were his two England strips, the discarded grey of Euro 96 which had been an eighth birthday present from Gran and the red one his Aunty Marie had bought in a July sale at the club shop.

A bit too much like Man U, thought Dave, wrinkling his nose with distaste. That's when it hit him, just how much football shaped his life. From the Premiership superstars wallpaper to the posters of his heroes in blue, from the scarves that festooned the headboard of his bed to the Everton bedspread, his whole room was a temple to the game. Then, in his mind's eye, he saw what was going to shape his life from then on, a rushing darkness and a boy lying twitching on the floor.

'Stupid!' Dave announced, kicking his programme box angrily against the far wall.

He spotted the photo George Rogan had taken of him at Bellefield and tugged it down from the wall. Life was mad. Why give you hopes if it had to go and dash them right away like this?

'Completely flipping stupid.'

He gripped the photo in both hands and made as if to rip it in two. That's when he felt a familiar drumbeat against his legs.

Thud thud thud.

He tousled Dixie's unruly fur. 'Sorry I shouted at you, lad,' he said, then gave a bitter laugh. Dixie. Even his dog's name came from the world of football. He was named after Everton's 60 goals-in-a-season all-time top scorer, Dixie Dean.

'I don't know,' sighed Dave, hugging the dog's neck. 'What do I do now, Dixie?'

By way of an answer Dixie wagged his tail even harder. *Thud thud thud.*

Dave looked at the photo and smiled. 'Those sleeves are ridiculous,' he told Dixie, squeezing the Blu-tak on the back. 'Good picture, though.'

Yes, it was a good picture. It had been a good dream, too, while it lasted. With a sigh, Dave flattened the photograph and stuck it back up.

Two

Four boys were on surveillance outside the Community Centre fence, Brain Damage, Costello, Tez and Jelly Wobble. The hard core. While the Diamonds enjoyed the sunlight of a bright spring evening, the gang glowered and plotted.

'What are you doing, Luke?' asked Brain Damage skidding his mountain bike to a stop.

'Counting,' said Costello.

'Counting what?'

'Diamonds, of course.'

'Eleven,' said Brain Damage. 'Lafferty and McGovern are missing. I already checked.'

'Well well,' said Costello. 'So what's come over you? Learning something from your Uncle Luke at last?'

'I counted the morons, that's all,' said Brain Damage. There were times when he really resented Costello's arrogance and this was one of them.

'We've won, Luke,' said Tez triumphantly.

'Too right,' said Jelly Wobble. 'We've got them crumbling at last.'

Costello listened to the exchange without speaking. Meanwhile, Tez was warming to his theme.

'They'll get tanked,' he crowed. 'Lafferty and McGovern are the ones who made them tick. They've no squad to speak of, either. They won't even have a substitute to put on the field if anyone gets injured.'

'Don't count your chickens before they're hatched,' said Costello. 'We did that over Jamie Moore that time. We thought the Diamonds were buried but they still bounced back. This time I'm taking out insurance.'

He took a printed leaflet out of his breast pocket and waved it.

'What's that?' asked Brain Damage.

'I told you: insurance.'

'No,' Brain Damage groaned. 'What is it *really*? What have you got there?'

'A fixture list,' said Costello.

'I don't get it …'

Costello winked at Tez and Jelly Wobble. 'Of course you don't, and that's what makes me the leader and you the … muscle.'

Tez and Jelly Wobble laughed right on cue. It didn't go down well with Brain Damage. He gave Costello a cool stare.

'You really want to know what I'm up to, don't you?' asked Costello.

Still smarting from the put-down, Brain Damage snarled the reply. 'I asked, didn't I?'

'Tomorrow,' Costello told him, 'Me and JW are off to our old stamping ground.'

Brain Damage looked blank. Which didn't surprise anyone.

'Kirkdale,' Costello explained.

'Yes,' said Brain Damage. 'I know Kirkdale. It's where you used to live. But ...'

'Would it help you if I mentioned Blessed Hearts Parochial Hall?'

'Blessed Hearts. As in the team you used to play for?'

'The same.'

'What for? I thought this was your patch now.'

'Oh, it is,' said Costello, eyeing the Diamonds practice session. 'But like I said, I'm taking out insurance.'

Brain Damage was determined to regain some sort of credibility. He didn't want to be just any gang member. He wanted to be a leader. 'That again!' he snorted. 'Do you have to talk in riddles?'

'It's only a riddle if you lack the brains to interpret it,' said Costello. Much to Brain Damage's irritation he winked at the other gang members. 'It's simple. Me and JW are renewing our interest in Blessed Hearts junior football club. We're still registered and they're desperate for players.'

'But I thought you'd dropped out,' said Brain Damage. 'Right after the Diamonds beat you.'

The jibe was meant to puncture Costello's arrogance, but he ignored it. 'We did,' he replied. 'But it's a good time to drop back in.'

Brain Damage shook his head. 'I give up. I haven't got a clue what you're on about.'

'Just read the fixture list,' said Costello, prodding at the sheet of paper. 'Read out the next match. This Sunday.'

'Blessed Hearts versus ...' Brain Damage's eyes lit up. In his enthusiasm for Costello's plan he put aside his jealousy and resentment. 'Luke, you're a genius.'

Costello chuckled. 'Of course.'

'Blessed Hearts,' Brain Damage announced to the gang, 'versus ... the Rough Diamonds.'

Three

The Diamonds players were taking it in turns to suck helium from the party balloons to make their voices go funny. All except Ratso, whose voice was funny anyway. They were laughing like hyenas.

'Go easy with that gas,' warned Dave Tasker. He managed the Community Centre and he'd collared the team after training to help him get the place ready for a mums and tots party. As the hysteria mounted he looked like he was regretting it. 'Where's our Kev, anyway?' he asked.

The Diamonds lowered their eyes. He'd touched a raw nerve.

'He didn't turn up,' said Bashir, stealing a glance at Ronnie who was talking on the pay phone in the foyer. 'He had a row with Ronnie.'

'Must have been some row,' said Dave, moving his step ladder along to pin up some bunting. 'He's been going on about getting through to the Cup final for ages. He doesn't seem to talk about anything else.'

'It's my fault,' said Jimmy.

'No it isn't,' said Daz. 'Guv should admit he was wrong. Having a punch-up with Brain Damage wouldn't solve anything.'

Joey jabbed his elbow into Daz's side.

'What's your game?' said Daz, massaging his ribs.

'I think Joey was trying to remind you that I'm Kev's uncle,' said Dave with a twinkle in his eye.

'Oh,' stammered an embarrassed Daz. 'I forgot.'

'Don't worry about it. This vendetta between Kev and Andy Ramage is nothing new.'

'No,' said Jamie, 'but Kev skipping training is.'

'That's right,' said Mattie. 'He ripped the back out of me and Carl when he thought we'd done it.'

'Do you want me to have a word?' asked Dave.

'Would you?' Gord answered eagerly.

'Don't get too excited,' said Ant. 'Guv's a stubborn so-and-so.'

'Don't I know it,' said Dave. 'I can't promise anything. He takes some shifting when his mind's made up.'

'Well,' Ronnie announced as he walked into the hall. 'I've just tried phoning Dave and Kevin. Dave's mum told me he's got an appointment at the hospital tomorrow ...'

'Hey,' said Jimmy. 'So's our Mike. He was telling me earlier.'

'That's right,' said Ronnie. 'I nearly forgot. It's his pain relief session, isn't it?'

Jimmy nodded. He looked suddenly thoughtful.

'But what about Lafferty?' asked John. 'We've got to get him back in the side. We've had it without him.'

Some of his team-mates rolled their eyes. Typical of Mr Misery to try to build morale like that.

'Forget it,' said Ratso. 'Dave's out of the picture. He signed forms for Everton, remember.'

'I'm not so sure,' said Ronnie. 'I think that's all on hold until we're clearer on his medical condition. George Rogan says there's no reason why Dave can't see the season out with us and take up his School of Excellence in September.'

'Does Dave know this?' asked Jimmy.

'He should do,' said Ronnie. 'George told his mum and dad the other day.'

'So what's his problem?' asked Joey.

'The little question of falling down all the rotten time,' said Mattie.

'And slobbering,' added Carl.

'Well, thanks for that helpful little thought,' said Ronnie. 'And who says kids these days aren't sensitive?'

'Well,' said Carl defensively. 'He did ... all over himself.'

'Oh, shut it, Carl,' said Jimmy. 'Your ignorance is showing.'

'So he can play?' asked John. 'You're telling us he can play.'

Ronnie shook his head. 'He could, lads, but he doesn't want to. He's worried ... or embarrassed. It's natural, really.'

There was a long silence.

'What about Guv?' asked Jamie. 'He was out when Bash and I called.'

'Same when I phoned,' said Ronnie. 'At least that's what his mum said.'

'You don't believe her, then?'

'I don't know, lad, but as far as I'm concerned the door's still open to him. If he wants to play he just has to turn up.'

'Can I tell him that?' asked Jamie.

'You can tell him,' said Ronnie, 'but I don't know if it'll do much good.'

A few heads drooped visibly. They knew the Guv'nor too well to be optimistic.

'Uncle Ron,' said Jimmy as the session broke up. 'Can I come back to yours?'

'Sure, run and phone your mum and tell her where you are.'

Jimmy was on his way to the phone when a thought occurred to Ronnie.

'Hang on,' he said. 'What are you actually coming round *for*?'

Jimmy paused. 'I want a word with Mike, that's all.'

As his nephew dialled home, Ronnie scratched his chin. The boy was up to something, but what?

Four

First the phone call, then the delegation. I saw Jamie and Bashir from my bedroom window. It didn't take a Sherlock Holmes to work out what they wanted. I was in for a bit of a surprise, though. I said something about Ronnie cracking first and wondered when he was going to apologize for taking me off. You know what? Jamie and Bash took Ronnie's side! They reckon I started it and thought I was dead tight getting my mum to lie about me being out when he called. I could hardly believe my ears. I mean, these were my two best mates talking. I thought that counted for something, but, oh no, all I got was earache over the barney with Costello and Co. To hear my mates talk you'd think I was the one trying to sabotage the Diamonds' Cup final hopes! Anyway, the three of us ended up sitting in stony silence. We were on a completely different wavelength and I was pretty sure it wasn't me who needed my signal adjusting.

So you won't change your mind? asks Bash.

Not until Ronnie apologizes, I tell him.

But it's our last league game, says Bash.

Then Ronnie had better bite the bullet, I tell him, and he'd better do it sharpish.

And you know what Jamie says? Hell will freeze over first.

Then up he gets and storms out. Like I've been a pain in the neck, or something. And that's not all. Jamie stops on the landing and turns round. You know what he said?

That I need to grow up.

Me!

Five

'Got a minute, Davey?' came a voice that Dave recognized.

'Mike,' said Dave. 'What are you doing here?'

'Waiting for you, you div.'

Dave gave him a puzzled look. Why was he a divvy?

'Well, that's the way it seems to me.' Mike glanced at Mrs Lafferty. 'Could I have a quick word with your Dave?'

Mrs Lafferty nodded. 'I'll nip over to the WRVS shop for a packet of chewing gum. Do you want anything?'

Dave shook his head. He was still wondering what made him a divvy.

'Everything OK?' asked Mike.

'What, with Mum?'

'No, you plank, with you.'

'Yes, I suppose. They say I don't have to come back.'

'Sounds good.'

Dave sighed. 'Too good. What do they know?'

'Quite a lot, really,' said Mike, smiling. 'It is a hospital, you know. So what's the score?'

'They think my medicine's about right,' Dave explained. 'Two tablets a day.'

'So what are you whingeing about all the time?'

How did you explain that medicine was no cure for voodoo? 'Whingeing, what do you mean?'

'You,' said Mike. 'Do you always give up this easily?'

Dave just stared.

'Well, have you had any more fits?'

'No.'

'So the tablets are working?'

'Yes, maybe.'

'No maybe about it.'

Dave thought of Brain Damage. Tablets? Big deal.

'Well, say something.'

Twice Dave had tangled with him and twice he'd had a fit. He pulled a face.

'Did I say something funny?' asked Mike. 'Come on, spit it out. What's to stop things getting back to normal?'

'I'm not though, am I … normal, I mean.'

'Why,' asked Mike, 'got another head somewhere round the back, have you? Started howling every full moon?'

'You know what I mean.'

'Oh, I know exactly what you mean,' said Mike. 'I've been there.'

Dave looked at Mike sitting in his wheelchair.

'That's what you mean, isn't it? Legs are normal. Wheelchairs aren't. I must be the world's expert in not being normal.'

'I never said you weren't normal.'

'No, you said *you* weren't. Amounts to the same thing, though.'

'It's different.'

'Of course it's different,' said Mike. 'Legs and brains, it's completely different. I take it you know what happened to me. You've heard the story?'

Dave nodded.

'I was a right young scally in my time,' said Mike. 'Nicking stuff, breaking windows. I even rode on a train roof once.'

'You never.'

'I did. Could have got myself fried. That was me, though. Thought I was invincible. Then this happened.'

'Fell through a roof, didn't you?'

'That's right,' said Mike. 'And I broke my back. Oh, I know I needed teaching a lesson but this …' He patted his legs. 'I didn't deserve this.'

Dave gave a smile of recognition. He wouldn't have minded a fiver for every time he'd said it. *It's not fair. I don't deserve it.*

'And that's how I was at first,' Mike continued. 'I just sat on my backside going on about how unfair it was.'

Dave didn't say a word. He'd been waiting for the pep talk, only he'd expected it from Ronnie.

'Then my old man lost his rag with me, asked me how long I was going to sit there like a big fat pudding. I hated him for that, I mean really hated him. How could he be so hard? Didn't he understand how I felt?'

Dave continued to listen in silence. What exactly did Mike want from him?

'In the end I suppose I just got fed up of watching Playbus and horse-racing. Or maybe it was the way people talked about me as if I wasn't there. *Marvellous, isn't he? Considering.* Anyway, I decided to do something. What is it they say? Get a life. See this?' He held out a medal on a ribbon. 'My latest basketball trophy. Good, eh?'

'Yes, Ronnie told us about it.'

'You're not impressed, then?'

'No,' said Dave. 'It's good.'

'Yes,' said Mike. 'It is actually. It's really good. You know what most people see when they meet me? The flipping wheelchair. But there's more to me than that, a lot more. And there's a lot more to you than a couple of fits. I got my head together and decided to sort myself out. So what about you?'

Dave saw his mum walking towards them. 'What about me?'

'How long are you going to keep this up, feeling sorry for yourself?'

'I'm not feeling sorry for myself!'

Mike snorted his disagreement. 'Could have fooled

me. You should have a video made. The Not Normal Kid.' Mike put on a whining voice. *Look at me, I had a couple of seizures. Don't you feel sorry for me?* That what you want to be when you grow up – a professional epileptic?'

'It's not like that!'

'No, well from where I'm sitting it looks just like that. Do you want to do this School of Excellence, or what?'

'Of course I do. It's my dream.'

'Then do it.'

Dave shook his head in disbelief. Mike, of all people, ought to understand.

'Don't shake your head at me, Dave,' said Mike. 'Just get out there and do it.'

Mrs Lafferty had joined them again.

'I'm right, aren't I, Mrs Lafferty?' Mike asked. 'There's nothing to stop him doing anything he likes.'

Mrs Lafferty turned towards Dave. She didn't seem too sure. 'No,' she said in a quiet voice.

'There's only one obstacle,' Mike continued confidently. 'You.'

Dave frowned. 'Ronnie put you up to this, didn't he?'

'My dad? He doesn't know anything about it. Actually, it was Jimmy's idea.'

A horn sounded. An ambulanceman was trying to get Mike's attention.

'That's my lift home,' said Mike, examining Dave's expressionless face. 'Looks like I've wasted my time, doesn't it?'

He wheeled himself over to the ambulance.

'Anyway,' he said, as the driver closed the rear door, 'let the lads know when you've stopped feeling sorry for yourself. They need you.'

Six

In the end, it was Costello and Brain Damage who got me to change my mind. Strange really because I'd convinced myself that Ronnie owed me an apology and no way was I about to back down. That's the way I am. Sorry isn't a word you'll find on any page of the McGovern English Dictionary. Let's face it, when did saying sorry do anybody any good? It just makes people think you're an easy touch. Anyway, about the change of mind, me and Jay were hardly even speaking after his visit. He seemed to be holding me responsible for just about everything that had happened.

That's how I ended up down the Ralla. The Diamond's got two railway lines, you see. First there's the Northern Line. Trains rushing by every ten or fifteen minutes into town. Then there's the Ralla, an old disused line overgown with about a million miles of mutant killer nettles. So I was sat there on the bridge lobbing stones at an old pram when I heard a familiar voice. It was Costello. Well, I wasn't about to get caught outnumbered four to one so I hopped over on to the Ralla at its highest point where there were a few patches of grass still free of nettles. And that's where I crouched while the gang walked past. Only they didn't walk past. They perched on the wall just like I'd done and started going on about how they'd smashed the Diamonds and how we'd never rise again. I was hidden just below them clenching my fists until the knuckles were completely white. They were boasting about the way they'd sorted me and Dave.

Them *sort* me, *I thought. No way.*

It was that clear. Suddenly I wasn't that bothered about Ronnie dropping me. He was still in the wrong, but it hardly seemed to matter any more. So the gang actually thought they'd got us beat, did they? That's what made my mind up, the idea of scumbags like that getting one over on me.

I'd chew my own leg off before I'd let that happen.

Ronnie, I thought as the gang moved off, it looks like it's time to kiss and make up.

Well, something like that.

Seven

'Well well,' said Ant, as he laced his boots. 'Look who it isn't.'

'Guv!'

Kev glanced round the changing-rooms. 'Where's Ronnie?'

'Putting up the goalposts with Jimmy and Gord,' Ratso answered. 'Why?'

'You're not still after that apology, are you?' asked Jamie.

'No.'

'You're ready to play?' asked Bashir.

'Yes.'

'Come to your senses then?' asked Daz.

Kev scowled as he unzipped his sports bag. 'Something like that. It is our last league game, after all.'

The other boys exchanged glances.

'So you admit you were in the wrong?' asked Daz.

Kev pulled his shirt on. 'Don't push it, all right?'

Daz grinned. 'Only winding you up, Guv.'

'So you're back?' asked Joey. 'For keeps?'

'I said so, didn't I?'

'Then let's play!'

'Ronnie won't like it,' said John gloomily.

'Don't be daft,' said Ratso. 'He'll be made up. You heard what he said: the door's still open. For Kev and Dave.'

'Hang on,' said Ant. 'Listen.'

They heard the sound of footsteps approaching.

Joey peeked out. 'It's him.'

A few seconds later Ronnie walked in. He spotted Kev immediately.

'Kevin,' he said, acknowledging the rebel's return.

'Ronnie,' said Kev.

Ronnie tossed a pair of boots to John. 'There you go. I've replaced that stud. Staying, Kevin?'

'Yes, staying.'

With that Ronnie was gone.

'That's it?' exclaimed Jamie, as the door closed. 'That's you and Ronnie making up?'

'Looks like it,' said Kev.

There were a few moments' silence, then everybody roared with laughter.

'Honestly,' said Daz, 'you pair would make a brick wall seem talkative.'

'I've said all I need,' Kev replied frostily. 'Now let's get out there and do the business.'

But he didn't. Do the business, that is.

'I'm what?' cried Kev, staring at the team sheet.

'Sub,' Ronnie answered. 'There's such a thing as loyalty. You weren't there on Monday night and Mattie was.'

All eyes were on Kev.

'He's going to do another runner,' John whispered to Bashir. 'I just know he is.'

Kev's face was bright red. He stared defiantly into Ronnie's eyes. 'So who's captain instead of me?'

'Here it comes,' said John. 'One runner.'

But it didn't come. Kev had just spotted the Blessed Hearts players taking the pitch.

'I don't believe it.'

Ronnie must have thought he meant the decision to

leave him on the bench. 'Well, you'd better believe it, Kev, because I'm not changing my mind. Ant's captain and you're sub and that's final.'

'Not that,' said Kev. 'Them.'

A few yards away, Costello and Jelly Wobble were doing stretches with the rest of the Blessed Hearts team to warm up. They greeted Kev with a sarcastic wave.

'Guv,' said Jamie. 'You're not clearing off again, are you?'

Kev stared back at Costello and Jelly Wobble, then at Brain Damage giving them the thumbs up from the touch-line.

'Oh, I'm staying,' said Kev. 'Wild horses wouldn't drag me away now.'

'What's the score?'

'Oh hello, Dave,' said Kev. 'I didn't expect to see you.'

'I could say the same about you,' Dave answered. 'Jimmy's been keeping me up to date about things.'

'Yes,' said Kev ruefully. 'I've been acting like a bit of a wally.'

'You and me both,' said Dave.

He noticed Mike looking at him but pretended not to.

'It's nil-nil,' said Kev. 'Are you playing, Dave?'

Dave clocked Brain Damage paying him his usual close attention and shook his head. 'I doubt it. I still feel a bit nervous.'

Kev nodded.

'Are we playing OK?' asked Dave.

'Not bad. But Costello and Jelly Wobble are getting away with murder. They're playing like animals. It was them who got me here, you know. Funny, isn't it? Sometimes it has to be the people you hate who show you what you have to do.'

As if to make the point, Costello dived in with a late challenge on Bashir, bringing him down in full flight.

'Oh, come on ref,' shouted Kev. 'Give us some protection.' He turned to Dave. 'See, that's why I came back. I can't let them break the Diamonds.'

Dave shook his head. 'So what's to stop them? At this rate somebody's going to get their leg broken.'

Kev frowned, then glanced at Brain Damage urging them on. 'They're trying to take our lads out of the final, aren't they?' he murmured.

'That's how it looks to me,' said Dave.

'We'd better tell Ronnie.'

'Somehow,' said Dave, 'I think he can work that out for himself.'

Ronnie was on the field remonstrating with the referee. Beside him, Bashir was rising to his feet and was gingerly testing his left ankle.

'One down,' Brain Damage hooted. 'Ten to go.' Then seeing Kev glaring at him, he shouted over, 'Hey, McGovern, get yourself on. I'm sure the lads would be glad to see you.'

'Don't rise to it,' said Dave.

Kev gave a slow motion nod. Dave wasn't at all sure Kev was going to be able to stay out of trouble. Hardly had play re-started when Costello did it again, this time clattering John from behind. The ref waved his arms, playing the advantage.

'Advantage!' roared Kev, 'after seeing a player flattened like that? You've got to be joking.'

Costello gave a sly grin. 'I'm enjoying this,' he said loudly.

The ref returned to him when the Diamonds' attack broke down, but Costello didn't look overly concerned. He got away with a telling off.

'Look at that,' said Kev. 'That deserved a booking, at least.'

'Tell me about it,' said Dave. 'But we've had this ref before, remember. He likes to keep play moving – at any price.'

On the stroke of half-time, Blessed Hearts were attacking. Jelly Wobble rose with Gord in the box. Shielded from the ref's gaze by a crowd of players he elbowed Gord in the face.

'Ref,' cried Kev. 'Foul, blatant foul.'

But play went on. Jelly Wobble's header was flicked on and Costello was there at the far post to volley it home.

One-nil.

'Bad news, eh lads?' said Mike, wheeling himself towards them.

'Disgusting,' said Kev. 'That ref's letting them do as they like.'

'How are you doing, Davey lad?' asked Mike. 'The old man was wondering if you'd like a game in the second half.'

'I don't know about that,' said Dave. 'I never even brought my kit.'

'Can't see that being much of a problem,' said Mike. 'Give it some thought.'

That's the trouble, thought Dave, I think too much and all that comes to mind is Brain Damage and the rushing darkness and the humiliation of lying there in front of your mates, completely out of it.

The Diamonds came back strongly, but once more Costello's spoiling tactics broke up the attack. This time Jimmy was the victim, scythed down by a tackle so vicious even this ref couldn't ignore it. Costello's name went into the book.

'Look at him,' said Kev, seething with frustration. 'He doesn't even care.'

'Of course not,' said Dave. 'He's loving every minute of it.'

Once again, Ronnie was on the field. Angry words passed between manager and referee.

'Dave,' called Mike, indicating the fallen Jimmy. 'Fancy that game yet?'

Dave looked at Brain Damage leading the rest of the gang in loud cheering as the half-time whistle blew. He remembered what Kev had said: Sometimes it's the people you hate who show you what you have to do. Got the power, have you? thought Dave. Well, maybe you're not the only one.

'You know what, Mike,' he said forcing back his fears, 'I might just take you up on that.'

Eight

'You're looking a bit down in the mouth, lads. What's the score?'

It was Nosmo. He'd taken the opportunity half-time gave him to check on Longmoor Celtic's Cup final opponents.

'One-nil,' grunted Ratso.

'Winning?'

'Losing.'

Nosmo couldn't disguise his pleasure. He smiled – a real cheesy, smirky grin. 'We're two-nil up against Ajax. You know what that means.'

Ratso nodded glumly. 'Keep that two-goal margin and you leap-frog over them on goal difference. You'll be champions.'

'That's right,' Nosmo gloated. 'And in seven days

when we lift the Cup we'll be double winners, too. First time anybody's done it.'

As Nosmo walked back to his own game, the Diamonds turned their attention to Ratso.

'That right?' asked Joey. 'Nobody's won the double before?'

'Not in the South Sefton League,' said Ratso. 'The competition's too fierce. Our league's always been a nursery of talent ...'

Joey rolled his eyes. Ratso was like the Encyclopaedia Britannica with zits.

'Ajax came closest last year,' Ratso continued. 'They had the championship in the bag, but Northend beat them on penalties in the Cup final.'

'At least we'll have been beaten by a decent side,' said John glumly.

'Listen, you,' Kev snarled. 'We're not going to get beaten. Where's Ronnie, anyway? We've got to get our tactics sorted.' He nodded in the direction of Jimmy and Bashir. Jimmy was rubbing his ankle and Bashir was nursing a gashed shin.

'Uncle Ronnie went to have a word with that ref,' said Jimmy. 'He isn't too happy.'

But Ronnie was no happier on his return.

'No luck?' asked Mike.

'No,' said Ronnie. 'The man won't listen. Asked me if I was aware football's a contact sport.'

'What did you say?'

'I tried to tell him that it's a contact sport *with rules*, but he wasn't prepared to listen.'

'So what do we do about this rotten fiasco?' asked Kev. 'At this rate we won't have a team for next Sunday.'

'The decision's made for me,' said Ronnie. 'Jimmy and Bash won't be playing any further part. Kev, you're on for Jimmy.'

'But who's going on for me?' asked Bashir.

'How's about it, Dave?' asked Ronnie. 'We're down to ten men. We need you. Call it your swan song.'

Dave glanced at Brain Damage and Costello. They were obviously having a laugh at the Diamonds' expense. More importantly, they were showing Dave what he had to do. Power? The Diamonds would think he was mad if he told them. 'You're on,' he said. 'I think I owe Brain Damage one.'

'Then get over to the changing-rooms,' said Ronnie. 'You'll have to wear Bashir's kit.'

'It'll be a tight fit,' said Dave.

'Well, it's that or nothing.'

Dave nodded and set off with Bashir.

'And make it snappy,' said Ronnie.

By the time Dave and Bashir got back, Ronnie was finishing his team talk. 'Ah, talk of the devil,' he said. 'Dave, I'll tell you what I told the rest of the lads. I know what's going on as well as you do. This Costello and his mate are out to crock as many of you as they can. A win today would be a bonus, but survival's the name of the game. I want that Cup. Just keep out of trouble. Ride their tackles if you can, but no matter how provoked you are, don't retaliate. Got that, Kev?'

Kevin nodded.

'Good.'

Ant started loosening the captain's armband.

'What are you doing, Anthony?' asked Ronnie.

'Giving Kev the skipper's armband.'

'Keep it on, son. Kev's got to earn it back.'

A few eyes darted in Kev's direction, but he accepted the decision without comment.

He set about regaining the armband in earnest, winning possession for the Diamonds right from the re-start.

'Guv, Guv,' shouted Dave as he ran into space. 'Long ball.'

Kev nodded and steadied himself to deliver the pass, and that's when Costello arrived, flattening his old enemy. To the Diamonds' relief and surprise, Kev simply got up and took the free kick quickly. He rolled it into John's path only to see Jelly Wobble bundle John to the floor. His tackle was even worse than Costello's.

'For crying out loud,' Ronnie was shouting from the touch-line. 'You've got to start giving out a few cautions, ref.'

The referee took a few paces towards the touch-line. 'I'd thank you to let me get on with my job,' he said. 'Bookings are at my discretion.'

'Then use it,' said Ronnie.

'The man's a couple of sheep short of a flock,' observed Mike, earning a stony glare from the referee.

'Call that a ref?' grumbled John as he picked himself up.

'What did you say, lad?' demanded the referee immediately. He was already nettled by Mike and Ronnie's heckling.

'Nothing.'

'Well, your nothing has just earned you a booking,' the referee told him. 'For dissent.'

The match official was suddenly surrounded by protesting Diamonds players.

'Come away,' yelled Kev. 'Or there'll be more of us in the book.'

But John was still arguing.

'O'Hara,' Kev shouted, dragging him by the shirt sleeve. 'Knock it off.'

John finally did as he was told.

'You should have taken control there,' Kev told Ant. 'If you're captain, you've got to get a grip.'

'I didn't want to be captain, remember,' said Ant. 'That was Ronnie's idea.'

Kev nodded and placed the ball for a free kick. Once again Dave had lost his marker. Travelling at speed, he took the ball to the edge of the penalty area and let fly with a first time effort that skimmed the crossbar. As he turned away, Costello came in with the worst challenge yet. As Dave got up, holding his knee, Costello hissed a warning into his face.

'That was just for starters, nutter. Next time you're going to stay down.'

'You tell him, Luke,' said Jelly Wobble. 'Had any funny turns lately, Lafferty? Been frothing at the mouth?' To make the point, he bubbled spittle on his lips. Dave could hear Brain Damage encouraging them from the touch-line.

'It won't be long now,' said Costello. 'Can't help yourself, can you, nutter?'

Dave stared back at them, but he didn't react. He wasn't going to give them the satisfaction. His anger wasn't a heat of the moment thing any more. It had turned cold as ice and hard like a clenched fist.

'We've got to do something,' said Ant, as play re-started.

'Are you going on about your long throw-in again?' asked Dave.

'No, not that.'

'What then?' asked Dave.

'Something to stop these tackles,' said Ant. 'They've got us by the short and curlies. If we defend ourselves or argue back we're the ones who get booked.'

'Leave it to me,' said Kev.

'Didn't you hear what Ronnie said?' Ant asked. 'Don't let the ref see you retaliate.'

Kev smiled. 'Who said I was going to let him *see*?' He

watched Luke gather the loose ball and launch a Blessed Hearts attack. 'Listen, lads, try to get the ref's attention.'

Dave nodded.

'I don't like the sound of this,' said Ant. 'Ronnie will go mad.'

'I'm not too happy either,' said Dave, 'but if we go on like this, there'll be no team left to face Longmoor next Sunday. This time I'm with Kev.'

Gord had just won the ball from Costello, but Costello chased him and hacked him down from behind.

Dave moved towards the action. 'You heard what Guv said. Let's do it.'

Ant nodded and followed him. Attracting the ref's attention was easy. Joey and Mattie were already complaining bitterly about the failure to book Costello. Dave and Ant just joined in, turning up the heat just enough to distract the ref without attracting a booking.

'Hey,' said Kev, taking immediate advantage of the uproar. 'Costello.'

As Costello turned, Kev stabbed a fierce punch into his ribs. It was a short jab, executed with hardly any swing but packed with power. Costello raised his head. Kev saw the wounded look and finished the job with a back hander across his enemy's face.

'You've had it now,' yelled Jelly Wobble as his friend crumpled to the turf with a cry.

Kev checked on the ref. He'd turned to see what had happened. Satisfied that the ref would witness Jelly Wobble's response, he waited for the punch. When it came he rocked back, but not so far that he avoided the blow entirely.

'Ugh.' Kev's fall could have won him an Oscar, and when he hit the deck he stayed there.

The ref had no option but to dismiss Jelly Wobble.

'No way!' shrieked Costello. 'He's the one who started it.' He was standing over Kev.

But the referee had had enough. 'I can only act on what I see.'

'Then see this,' bawled Costello, beside himself with anger.

Kev saw the kick coming and braced himself. By grabbing Costello's ankle, he took most of the force out of it.

'Right,' said the referee, as Kev doubled up like he'd been mortally wounded. 'You're off, as well.'

'Keanu Reeves has got nothing on the Guv'nor,' murmured Dave appreciatively.

Jelly Wobble and Costello saw the look of satisfaction on the faces of the Diamonds players and realised they'd been had.

As they left the pitch, Dave bent over Kev. 'You OK, Guv?' he asked.

'Yes,' said Kev, grinning up at him. 'Never better. Now let's finish the job.'

Nine

Next evening the Diamonds were in jubilant mood. Not only had they come away from the Blessed Hearts game with two-one win, they'd also foiled Costello's plan and made a complete show of him. Even the presence of the gang on the other side of the Community Centre fence didn't faze them.

'Look at them,' said Ant. 'They're beaten.'

'Don't write them off yet,' said Kev, teeing up a shot for Jamie. 'A tiger is at its most dangerous when it's wounded.'

Dave laughed out loud. 'Where did you dig up that little gem?' he asked.

'Our Gareth's comic,' said Kev, blushing.

Dave looked around the Community Centre field. His last training session with the Diamonds, soon to be followed by his last match for them. He could feel the edges of the letter sticking into his leg. Every time he changed into a new set of clothes he would transfer his letter. Like a magic talisman.

'Dave,' shouted Daz. 'Hit a few towards the top corner.'

Dave obliged, netting two on the run before Daz finally palmed one over.

'Sharp tonight, aren't you?' panted Daz.

Dave smiled. Of course he was sharp. It had come in the post that morning. The letter confirming that the offer of the School of Excellence had had to take his medical condition into consideration but would now begin in September.

'And another,' said Daz.

Dave nodded and struck a crisp shot past Daz.

'OK,' the keeper conceded. 'I know when I'm beaten. Swop with Jamie.'

Dave obliged and started teeing up shots for his strike partner.

'Think we can win this Sunday, Guv?' Dave asked Kev.

'Sure,' said Kev. 'Why not?'

Dave shrugged. 'Be a turn-up if we do,' he said, 'considering the state we were in last autumn.'

Kev nodded. 'Licking boys, weren't we? Well, not any more, Davey lad. Longmoor have got the league title, but they're not going to do the double. Not when we're in their way.'

'So how do we stop them?' asked John, stopping to listen. 'They walloped us a fortnight ago.'

'We were under strength, then,' said Kev. 'We'll have a full squad on Sunday.'

'Sure you're up to it?' John asked Dave.

'Of course he's up to it,' said Jimmy. 'Aren't you, Dave?'

'I don't see why not,' said Dave. 'I haven't had a seizure …' He gave Brain Damage a wary glance. 'Not since they showed up at school.'

'You don't think the gang can bring them on, do you?' asked John.

'Don't be stupid,' said Jimmy, defending his mate.

'Seems funny though, doesn't it?' interrupted Mattie. 'I mean, both times you've keeled over, Costello was there.'

'Yes,' said Carl. 'It makes you think.'

'Since when did you and thinking go together?' snapped Kev. He noticed that Dave had gone suddenly quiet. 'You're talking rubbish.'

'All right,' said Mattie. 'Keep your hair on, will you?'

'Yes, and if you can't think of anything sensible to say,' Kev snarled. 'Just keep your gob shut.'

Mattie and Carl took the none too subtle hint and walked away. Soon Kev, Jimmy and Dave were left alone.

'Well?' said Kev.

'Well what?'

'You don't believe their gobbledygook, do you?'

'What, about them bringing on my seizures?'

'Of course he doesn't,' said Jimmy.

'Jim,' said Kev coolly. 'I was asking Dave.'

Dave looked at where the gang had been standing, but they'd gone. 'No,' he said. 'I don't.'

But something in his voice made Kev uneasy.

The gang had retreated to the top of Owen Avenue by the time Kev asked his question.

'We'll have one last try,' said Costello. 'Your way.'

'I thought you might say that,' Brain Damage leered. He clenched his fist. 'Always comes down to this in the end.'

Costello nodded. 'Let's just make sure we get him,' he said. 'We won't get another chance.'

Ronnie called the boys together at half past seven. 'Listen up,' he said. 'Here's the team for Sunday.'

As he rattled through the names Kev and Dave smiled. They were in at the expense of Carl and Mattie.

'I'm starting with our strongest side,' said Ronnie.

'You can say that again,' murmured Jamie. He was glad to see the Guv'nor back.

'Just a little word on the question of the team captain,' Ronnie continued.

Kev stared ahead, ignoring the glances of his team-mates.

'Kev and I have had our disagreements, but we all know how much we need his presence. And by the way …' He gave a sly grin. 'That was a cute move yesterday, the way you turned the tables on those young thugs.' He paused for a second. 'Not that I saw anything, of course.'

'Heaven forbid,' said Ratso.

Ronnie winked before adding: 'Kev lad, you've got the skipper's arm band back. You've earned it.'

Ten

Praise from Ronnie. Whatever next! So you need me now, do you? It's always the way, isn't it? Everybody takes a pop at you until their backs are against the wall, then it's 'Kev McGovern, come on down.' Well, I'll be there for the Final, all right, only I'm doing it my way. Football's war. Always has been, always will. Oh, everybody remembers the Dave Laffertys, the natural talents, the glory boys. But you need more than skill to win trophies. You need sweat and muscle and the will to win. You've got to want that trophy so much you could cry. That's where I come in. Fire, passion, anger. Total commitment.

People are going to remember Dave. They always do. They'll remember the way he traps the ball, the footwork, the headers, the shots. You know what they'll remember about me? The sheer determination, the readiness to run myself into the ground. I'll cover so much of that pitch they'll think there's two of me.

It could be the last time Dave and I play together in a Diamonds shirt, but don't go shedding any tears. This is going to be special, the stuff legends are made of. The Rough Diamonds, the team that rose from the bottom of the league in a single season and lifted the Challenge Cup. My fire to light the flame. Dave's spells to work the magic. The two hearts are beating again.

Eleven

Dave flicked a nervous glance out of the passenger-side window. It was at times like this when you were glad of a lift in the car. The two-minute drive from home didn't seem so silly any more.

As Dad pulled into Jacob's Lane car park, Brain Damage led the gang's rush. 'Coo-ee,' he called. 'Not feeling dizzy, are you, Lafferty?'

An instant later, Costello and Tez Cronin had joined him, pressing their faces against the window. They were smearing it with white froth. Dave scowled. The shaving foam trick again. Didn't they ever let up?

'Oi,' shouted Dad, lowering the window. 'Clear off.'

The gang retreated a few steps but kept up their antics. Dave wanted to fade into the upholstery. Soon they were taking it in turns to do shaky walks across the car park.

'Are they doing what I think they're doing?' asked Dad. 'Is that for your benefit?'

Dave nodded. 'It's all right, Dad. I can handle it. It's been going on for weeks.'

'Why didn't you say?' asked Mum. 'Some things you shouldn't have to handle.'

Dad was less composed. 'Twisted little beggars,' he ranted. 'I'll give them what for …'

'Leave it,' said Mum. 'You'll only enourage them. That's what they want – for us to react.'

'I'll react, all right,' said Dad. 'I'll react right across their lugholes. That's the Ramage boy, isn't it? The one who—'

'Mum's right,' said Dave, interrupting. 'Just ignore it, Dad. That's what I do.' He said it convincingly enough. He just wished it was that easy.

'Come on,' said Mum. 'Let's get you into the changing-rooms. There are more pressing things than a handful of hooligans. The best thing you can do is score the winning goal today. That'll wipe the smile off their stupid faces.'

Dave was glad of Mum's company that Sunday morning. There had been times over the last few weeks when she'd driven him mad over his 'problem', but somehow she always managed to come good in the end.

'Hey, Lafferty,' shouted Costello, as Dave made his way to the changing-room door, 'Got your bodyguards with you today?'

'It won't save you from me,' said Brain Damage. 'Don't forget. I have the power.'

'What did he mean by that?' asked Mum.

'Just talk,' said Dave.

And he was sure it was. But he could never quite get the idea out of his mind. It was always there, nagging away at the back of his mind. The worry about the rushing darkness. The doubt.

The Diamonds took the field to the tune of 'Naked' by Louise. Somehow, it wasn't the kind of motivating anthem they'd come to expect blaring out of Ratso's ghetto blaster. 'Simply the Best' or 'We are the Champions' maybe. But 'Naked'?

'What in the name of Scooby Doo has that got to do with footy?' asked Ant, as the rest of the side came to a halt and stood gaping in disbelief.

'Nothing,' said Ratso guiltily. 'I put the tape in the wrong way round. Sorry.'

The Longmoor players were laughing themselves silly.

'Nice one,' said Nosmo. 'So when do you start the striptease?'

'Yes,' shouted Costello. 'Time to get your kit off, Diamonds.'

'But watch you don't start slobbering, Lafferty,' added Brain Damage.

'Oh, nice one, Ratso,' said John. 'A good start, that is.'

'John,' said Kev. 'Can it, will you? You're not helping.'

'Yes,' said Ant. 'Give us all a break and go and moan somewhere else.'

'You know what?' said Nosmo. 'I really do wish we'd had that bet. You're going to get buried.'

Skinhead grinned and drew a finger slowly across his

throat. 'Rough Diamonds RIP.'

Ratso pressed the stop button on his ghetto blaster. 'Sorry, lads.' Then a feeble attempt at a joke. 'It could have been worse. I've got the 'Birdy Song' on here somewhere.'

But nobody was listening. The Diamonds' triumphal entry had turned into a humiliating farce.

'A bit of a hiccup,' Kev was telling his team-mates. 'That's all it was. We've still got the beating of this team. We've done it before.'

Nosmo and Skinhead led the derisive laughter. The Diamonds weren't too positive, either. The sentiment was right but nobody looked convinced. Their mid-season three-two victory had been completely overshadowed by the recent eight-one drubbing.

'Right,' said Kev, sensing the lack of response. 'Let's play.'

If he'd had a sneak preview of the first ten minutes he might not have been so keen. Longmoor ran the show right from the kick-off with Nosmo and Skinhead muscling the Diamonds' midfield off their game.

'Come on,' Kev yelled at John and Bashir. 'We're going to have to fight for every ball.'

But it was an unequal contest. Longmoor were brimming with confidence after winning the league title. They were quicker on to the ball, sharper into the tackle and more committed in attack. In contrast, the Diamonds could barely get started. Bashir had just set off on one of his line-hugging runs when Nosmo wrapped his leg round the ball and came away with it.

'Get back, get back,' Kev roared seeing the danger of a lightning raid down the wing.

Joey tried to get in a challenge but Nosmo simply lengthened his stride and went past him. Steadying himself, the Longmoor skipper slipped the ball through

Gord's legs as he came out. Skinhead had no problem slotting it home.

One-nil to Longmoor.

'They're going to give us another rotten hiding,' groaned John.

'Either he shuts his mouth,' Ant fumed, 'or I'll shut it for him.'

'Knock it off,' said Kev, realising he had to get a grip of things. And quickly. 'There's no point arguing among ourselves. It's only one goal.'

But not for long. First, the Diamonds lost their way up front. Dave had got his first clear sight of goal when Brain Damage sprang from a knot of spectators. Having taken his eye off the ball, Dave scuffed it badly, letting it roll softly to the keeper.

'What do you call that?' Ant demanded. 'You usually put chances like that away, no problem.'

'Sorry,' said Dave.

It was an overused word with the Diamonds that morning.

'What use is sorry?' grunted Ant. 'Sort yourself out.'

The gang's laughter was still ringing in Dave's ears when the Longmoor goalie punted the ball right into the Diamonds penalty area.

'Mine,' shouted Daz, but Gord had already committed himself to the challenge. Before Daz had a chance to recover the miscued header was in the back of the net.

'What's wrong with you, Gord?' cried Daz. 'Didn't you hear me call?'

'Sorry.'

'Next time I say mine,' Daz continued regardless, 'I mean *mine*. You leave it, OK?'

'I said sorry, didn't I?'

But it was an unforgiving Daz who stamped away, still muttering to himself.

'This is terrible,' said Bashir.

'Embarrassing,' Dave agreed. He saw his parents watching from their vantage point by the corner flag at the Longmoor end. Mum waved cheerfully. Dad, who knew a bit more about football, gave a wan smile. He knew what Dave was going through.

'Here they come again,' said John as yet another Diamonds attack broke down.

Skinhead was on the ball. A third goal looked on the cards as he dummied Ant, but Gord was alive to the danger and came in with a crunching tackle.

'That's more like it,' said Daz. 'Well done, Iron Man.'

Gord nodded ruefully. He was still smarting from the own goal.

'Come on, lads,' urged Kev as he brought the ball out of defence. 'You haven't forgotten, have you? This is the Cup final, for goodness sake.'

Noticing Dave making a run ahead of him he nutmegged the oncoming defender and released the ball.

'Nutter!' was the chorus from the gang as Dave ran on to it.

'Oh Dave,' groaned Kev.

Not for the first time, Dave had fluffed a promising chance.

'Sorry, Guv.'

'You're not letting that shower get to you, are you?' asked Kev.

Dave shook his head, but he wasn't fooling anybody. It suddenly felt as if Brain Damage did have the power, after all.

'Forget it,' said Kev. But his voice sounded flat.

In the next five minutes Dave was twice guilty of failing to control the ball in promising situations. He noticed with a sinking heart that Kev was looking towards Ronnie.

'What's up, Dave?' hissed Jimmy. 'This is the final. Uncle Ronnie will pull you off if you don't buck up. George Rogan's watching, you know.'

Dave glimpsed Costello and Co trying to catch his attention. They were giving the thumbs down. He was having a nightmare and they were loving every minute of it.

'Nobody's taking me off,' Dave announced defiantly.

'So you're going to pull yourself together?' asked Kev, eavesdropping on the exchange. 'Do what you were born for? Weave the magic?'

Sometimes that's all it takes to turn things round. The right combination of threats and encouragement. Ronnie was ready to wield the axe, but Kev was there with exactly the right words. *Do what you were born for. Weave the magic.* Dave felt a surge of power. *His* power. Then it was burning in his veins, the cocky self-confidence, the irrepressible will to win.

'Just watch me.'

He was as good as his word. Blocking out the continuing barracking by the gang, he started to get into the game, completing a couple of telling passes and narrowly missing with a long-range shot.

'More like it,' said Kev. 'We'll turn this round yet.'

But Longmoor weren't about to fold under the first spell of sustained pressure from the Diamonds. When their keeper punched out a weak shot from John, the break was on. With half a dozen players thrown into attack, the Diamonds were suddenly stretched at the back.

'Ant,' yelled Kev. 'Nosmo's unmarked. Get on him.'

It was easier said than done. Skinhead played a perfect first-time ball to the far post. Nosmo only had to nod it home from close range.

Three-nil down.

'We've really had it now,' said John.

'You have, you mean,' Ant snarled. 'One more comment like that and I'll bladder you.'

'Oh, cut it out,' groaned Kev, as he dribbled the ball back to the centre circle. 'They're laughing at us.'

It was true. Longmoor were loving every minute of the wrangling between the Diamonds players. So were the gang.

'Told you I had the power,' yelled Brain Damage. He was jubilant.

'I'll show you whose got the flipping power,' Dave said under his breath. 'Kev,' he whispered. 'Hold it for a sec, then knock it over the top for me.'

With that, he hared off down the middle of the pitch, leaving his markers for dead. As Kev's long ball dropped, Dave was able to take it down with his instep and find Jamie with a first-time pass. Jamie stabbed it home with glee.

'Three-one,' said Kev. 'A two-goal deficit. It isn't over yet.'

But as the ref blew the half-time whistle he saw his team-mates' faces. Magic or no magic, they looked beaten already.

Twelve

As the Diamonds flopped disconsolately on the ground, Ronnie stood silently, his arms folded over his chest. Of the players only Kev and Dave were on their feet. They were too pumped up to keep still.

'Feeling generous, are you?' Ronnie asked. 'You've become Longmoor Celtic fans all of a sudden?'

'While Kev and Dave paced up and down, the rest of

the side lowered their eyes. Nobody wanted to meet the manager's gaze.

'John King will have to do a bit of body-building,' Ronnie continued. 'After all, that's two pieces of silverware he'll be holding at the presentation evening.'

It was Kev who finally responded. 'OK OK,' he sighed. 'We get the message. You're right, Ronnie, we're handing them the double on a plate.'

'But what do we do about it?' asked Jimmy. 'They're running us ragged.'

'You compete,' said Mike, beating Ronnie to it. 'You show a bit of pride. You don't get these ...' he held up his basketball medals, '... for surrendering. If you want to win things then you've got to fight for them. Tell me, do you want that Cup?'

There was a heavy silence.

'I said, do you want that Cup?'

'Of course we do,' Bashir replied. 'I want to shut *them* up.' He was looking at the gang. 'I want to pay them back for the names they call me.'

'And what's the best way to do it?' asked Ronnie

No answer.

'Well?'

'Win the game,' said Bashir quietly.

Ronnie cupped a hand behind his ear. 'What was that?'

'Win the game,' said Bashir.

'Right,' said Ronnie, taking over from Mike. 'Now you're talking. But it's only words. What I want is action. Listen, I know these lads are all a year older than you. They're bigger, stronger too, but they're not better. You know you can beat them. You've done it before. You've just got to play like you mean it.'

'But how?' asked John.

'For a start,' said Ronnie, 'you're giving them too

much space. They're running at you and you're just backing off. You're defending too deep.'

'So we push up?' asked Kev.

'Too right you push up,' said Mike, diving in again. 'You're defending right in front of your own goal. You should be starting to break up their attacks on the half-way line.'

'And you're not thinking,' said Ronnie. 'Take you, Ant. Match after match you've been going on about your long throws. Now that we need them, what do you do? You forget all about it. And you, Dave, don't just stand there waiting for the ball. Leave Jamie to play up front for once. Drop off and help John and Kev in midfield. As for you Daz ...'

The goalie looked dumbstruck. Ronnie was actually going to criticize *him*!

'You've got a terrific kick on you but you've hardly used it. Vary the service you're giving the outfield players. Don't throw it out to the wing-backs all the time. Longmoor have sussed that, and they're dispossessing our lads thirty yards from our own goal line. Sometimes look up and just launch it.'

'So you think we can get back into it?' asked Dave, warily clocking the gang's activities.

'Trust me,' Ronnie replied with a reassuring wink. 'I know it.'

Five minutes into the second half, and Nosmo was feeling the pressure. He shoved Dave roughly in the chest. 'I'll have you for that.'

'Knock it off,' said Dave. 'That was a fair challenge.'

'Fair?' exclaimed Skinhead as he joined the fracas. 'Look at his knee, will you?'

'That's enough, lads,' said the ref. 'I saw nothing

untoward. I've awarded a throw-in to the Rough Diamonds. Now play on.'

'What was all that about?' asked Dave, genuinely
shocked at Nosmo's reaction. 'That was no foul.'

'I'll tell you what that was about,' said Kev. 'Them
getting rattled, that's what.'

Dave smiled. 'You reckon?'

'Trust me,' said Kev. 'We're getting to them.'

Longmoor still had the better of possession, but only
just. The swagger had gone out of their play. They no
longer had the time on the ball they had enjoyed in the
first half. Everything they did was rushed and always
contested by a ready Diamonds challenge.

'Now?' asked Ant, as Ratso ran for the ball.

'Now,' said Kev.

As Ant rubbed moisture off the ball, Jamie and Dave
made decoy runs, which drew the Longmoor defenders.
Bashir was left unmarked on the far post. Spotting the
little winger in space, Ant took a short run up and
propelled the ball with pin-point accuracy to Bashir's
feet. Realizing the danger too late, the Longmoor
defenders were feverishly scrambling to block him, but
Bashir wasn't hanging about for the tackle. He drove the
ball in low. Checking his run, Dave threw himself into the
air, managing to volley the ball in from waist height.

Only three-two down.

'Goal-azzo!' shrilled Ratso.

'Brilliant, Davey lad,' said Kev. 'You too, Bash.'

'And don't forget who started it,' said Jamie, nodding
in Ant's direction.

Longmoor immediately returned to the attack, but the
Diamonds defence was equal to the task, doubling up on
Nosmo to snuff out the main danger.

'Gord,' called Dave as the centre-back came away
with the ball. 'Run it.'

Revelling in the space Longmoor were giving him, Gord drove forward strongly. Dave jinked and zig-zagged ahead of him, leading his marker a merry dance.

'Give it to Dave,' shouted Kev.

Gord glanced at the striker but the frown on Dave's face told him to hold on to the ball. Finding himself just twenty yards out Gord decided to shoot. Cries of *Ooh* greeted a drive that cannoned off the bar. But there were louder shouts still for what happened next. Dave brought the ball down on the penalty spot and fired it back in. Goal.

Three-all.

'Priceless,' said an admiring Kev. 'An absolute peach.'

'Thanks,' said Dave, but he was hardly listening. He was staring at the penalty spot beneath his feet. What *would* happen if a penalty were awarded? He gave Brain Damage a cold stare then jogged upfield for the re-start.

'We're back on terms,' said Kev. 'Now concentrate.'

The Diamonds did better than concentrate. They dispossessed Longmoor and went straight back on to the attack. This time the chance fell to Jamie who hit the angle of bar and post.

'Hard luck,' said Kev.

There was harder luck to come. The Longmoor keeper bounced the ball twice then belted it back upfield. Gord rose to head it away only to be pushed from behind.

'Foul!' claimed Ant, but the ref had been unsighted.

'Aw, ref!'

The official brushed aside the Diamonds' complaints and waved play on. Having anticipated a free kick, the Diamonds defence was caught napping. A skilful exchange of passes between Skinhead and Nosmo and the Longmoor skipper was clear just four yards out. He made no mistake with the clear shot on goal.

Four-three to Longmoor.

'Only three minutes left,' shouted Ronnie, tapping at his watch.

The Longmoor goal was under permanent siege from then on. First Dave had a header plucked out of the goalmouth by the Longmoor keeper. Claims that it had crossed the line were ignored, much to the delight of Brain Damage.

'You've had it, Lafferty,' he gloated.

But it wasn't over yet. Kev was next to go for goal with an athletic bicycle kick that only narrowly cleared the bar. Thirty seconds later, Jamie fired in a shot from a tight angle only to see it cleared on the line by Nosmo.

'Thirty seconds,' said Ronnie, haring down the touchline to where Ant was shaping up for the throw-in. 'Vary it, Anthony.'

Ant nodded. Seeing a cluster of Longmoor players protecting the far post, he whipped the ball in low and hard towards the nearside upright. Dave was the first to move, meeting it with a glancing header. Nosmo made a despairing attempt at a second clearance only to smash it into the roof of his own net. As he crumpled to the ground with his head in his hands, Dave went off on a victory run.

'Brilliant, Davey,' shouted Mum.

'Yes, nice one, son,' said Dad. 'Now get down there and hit the winner.'

Dave laughed. 'Don't want much, do you, Dad?' Pausing only to give Brain Damage and the gang a sarcastic wave, Dave ran to join Kev and Jamie in the centre circle.

'We're in injury time,' said Kev. 'Looks like it's going to extra time.'

Nosmo didn't look too happy with the prospect. He was breathing heavily and seemed so heavy-legged that he couldn't even re-start the match.

'You look like you've been in a game now,' said Kev. 'Still want that bet on the outcome, Nos?'

Nosmo glared and hit the ball angrily at the Diamonds captain. Kev wasn't one to look a gift horse in the mouth and set off gleefully downfield. He saw the whistle in the ref's mouth. No time for any fancy stuff. He powered forward, beating Skinhead then hurdling a tired challenge by one of the Longmoor centre-backs before driving on into the penalty area. Drifting left to go round the goalie, Kev steadied himself for the shot. That's when he felt the keeper's hand tugging his ankle. As he tumbled to the ground a roar went up.

'Penalty!'

Kev was on his feet in an instant. 'Dave. Where are you? Jamie, you seen Dave?'

The Diamonds' nominated penalty-taker seemed to have gone walkabout.

'Anybody seen Dave?' Kev asked.

'I'm here, Guv,' said Dave, reluctantly edging away from the touch-line. He could hardly breathe, never mind answer. So it had come down to this. He was aware of the gang making their way behind the Longmoor goal to put him off.

'Ready, Dave?' asked Kev. 'Nothing fancy. Remember what Gareth Southgate's mum said after Euro 96. Just hit it.'

Dave nodded. As he placed the ball, he tried to shut everything out. Tried and failed. Brain Damage was leading the gang doing shaky walks behind the goal. The shaving foam had come out again. Dave's eyes narrowed. If he fluffed his kick he would never be free of their taunts.

Focusing on the ball, he took three steps back. A quick glance at goal then three more backward steps. Suddenly there was no Brain Damage, no gang, no watching crowd, no problem. Just him and the ball in a tunnel that started at the instep of his right boot and ended in the back of the net. No friends, no enemies, no seizure, no power. Him and his gift.

'Hit it!' bawled Kev.

But Dave didn't hear. He was already over the ball, striking it fiercely into the left-hand corner.

'Goal!

And that was it. Mayhem. The world seemed to fall in on him. It was only as he raised his face from the pitch, spitting out turf and grass, that he realized he was at the bottom of a scrum of delirious Diamonds players. They'd won. Five-four.

'Let him up,' said Jimmy anxiously. 'You never know.'

'Don't worry about me,' said Dave. 'I've got it under control. I've got *everything* under control.'

As if to make his point he ran to Brain Damage.

'Hey you,' he said. 'Ugly.'

Brain Damage stared back.

'Who's got the power now?'

No answer.

'I have, Brain Damage. I have.'

Thirteen

It's been a great night. The presentation of the League and Cup trophies was down at the Dockers' Club. George Rogan did the honours. Everybody was there. Well, nearly everybody. Dad didn't show, of course, but what's new about that? He'd miss his own funeral. Longmoor were up first to collect the Championship shield. Nosmo hoisted it above his head. His dad was clambering over everybody to video the moment. Nos had this big smile on his face. Until he saw us watching, that is. I think we spoiled the party a bit when we won the Cup last Sunday.

Then it was our turn to walk to the front to collect our trophy. Normally, I would have led the lads up to the top table, but it didn't seem right somehow. I realized that it was Dave who should lift the Cup. How better could we say thanks for everything he'd done for the Diamonds? He argued with me for a moment or two, of course, but he was made up, really. You should have seen him standing there with this big silver Cup in his arms. King of the League, that's Davey. I always knew he was better than that Achilles feller. Dave had his weakness, but he didn't let it beat him. He came through. I'm still sort of jealous, I suppose. Who wouldn't be when you're always getting compared to Boy Wonder? There he was with his perfect mum and dad holding hands beside him. But he's a mate so I dare say I'll learn to live with it. I hope the School of Excellence works out for him. I've got a feeling it will. I can just see Dave turning out at Goodison.

So that's about it. At the end of the evening I found myself standing on Townsend Avenue, waiting for the bus with Mum and our Gareth. I couldn't help looking round to see if Costello and Brain Damage were about, but they'll be keeping their heads down. For a while, anyway.

So that's it, our first season's over. It started with us rooted to the bottom of the league and ended with us winning the Cup. Pretty impressive, eh? But am I satisfied yet? Don't you believe it! Remember Everton's club motto: Nil satis nisi optimum. *Nothing but the best, to those of you who can't read Greek. Or is it Latin? Who cares? I'm writing my own language now. It isn't easy, finding the words to say who you are, but I'm getting there. When I moved to the Diamond I was no more than a two-bit scally, feeling sorry for myself and taking a pop at anybody who got in my way. I'm no angel now, but I'm learning to handle myself, knowing when to dive in and knowing when to back off. A few months ago it was me against the world. Now I've got a bunch of mates and I'm starting to feel I'm part of something, a big part. Next season we'll be older, more confident in our own abilities. Stronger in every way. I tell you, the sky's the limit.*

Some You Win ...

'There's me with my mind full of the beautiful game ... and what are we really – a bunch of deatbeats ...'

But Kev has a reputation to live up to and when he takes over as captain of the Rough Diamonds he pulls the team up from the bottom of the league, and makes them play to win ... every match.

Under Pressure

'The pressure's on. Like when you go for a fifty-fifty ball. Somebody's going to blink, and it isn't me. Ever.'

Kev, captain of the Rough Diamonds, acts swiftly when too many of the lads just aren't playing the game and let pressures off the pitch threaten the team's future.

Divided We Fall

'If you don't take risks you're nothing. There's only half an inch of space between determination and dirty play and I live in it.'

That's the law Kev McGovern lays down for the Rough Diamonds on the pitch, but what about off it? When Kev's best mate Jamie's world is wrecked by dirty play he's desperate to get everything back to safe, reliable normality.